DARK MINDS PRESS

NAMING THE BONES

Published by
Dark Minds Press
31 Gristmill Close
Cheltenham
Glos.
GL51 0PZ
www.darkmindspress.com
Mail@darkmindspress.com
First Print Edition – July 2017
Cover Image © 77studios
www.77studios.blogspot.com
The copyright of this story
remains the property of the author.
Interior layout by Anthony Watson

ISBN-13: 978-1544177748
ISBN-10: 1544177747

DARK MINDS NOVELLAS

5

NAMING THE BONES

A novella

by

Laura Mauro

For Grandad Pat,

Who always said London was the best city
in the world.

ONE

First, there was darkness.

There were other things too: burning, and frantic motion, and people crying somewhere very far away. But the darkness came first. A profound, abrupt blackness, depthless as the abyss and thick, the airless texture of oil in the back of the throat. For a long, still moment Alessa thought she might have gone suddenly blind, that something deep inside her brain had irrevocably short-circuited.

Then the emergency lights finally came on, bathing the carriage in weak yellow. And only then did Alessa rise from her seat - slowly, because some distant part of her seemed to hurt very much - and survey the chaos around her. With a terrible lack of urgency she picked her way through thick debris; gnarled fingers of metal hung from the ceiling, the remains of handrails clutched by gloved hands only five minutes earlier. It seemed that Alessa was moving in a near-silent dream: the only sound was a murky static fuzz, the only motion the occasional flicker of the lights overhead and her shambling progress, sleepwalker-slow. Scattered piles of upholstery cluttered the floor like discarded laundry; a blizzard of broken glass lay atop them, yellow as old teeth in the pale light. Her feet caught in the snarls of fabric as she progressed, conspiring to trip her over; she tugged her foot away irritably, surrendering one high-heel.

There was only one other person in the carriage, though she was sure there had been others just minutes before. A woman sat at the far end with her hands folded in her lap, staring serenely out of the ruined window opposite; her gaze was fixed so thoroughly on the empty windowframe that she did not notice Alessa approach.

Alessa pushed forward. The air itself seemed solid, an invisible mass meeting her progress with unlikely resistance; it tasted of dust, and of copper, a thick glut pushing down into her lungs, pooling slowly in the thickets of bronchioli.

Alessa reached out a hand. Her fingers brushed the woman's shoulder; the fur trim of her parka was damp beneath Alessa's fingers. She tugged lightly, seeking the woman's attention, but she kept on staring, dark eyes wide and unblinking. Her lips were slightly parted, as if she'd been about to speak before the darkness enveloped them both and had forgotten what she was going to say.

"Excuse me," Alessa said hesitantly.

The woman moved slowly, pale moon-face turning up to meet Alessa's. It was only then that Alessa noticed the constellation of glass fragments embedded in her cheek, glittering studs travelling in a slow arc upwards, and the dark crater of blood welling up beneath each individual shard. One unsteady hand moved up, seeking Alessa's hand, grasping her fingers; her skin was slick with gore.

"You're bleeding," the woman said, in wide-eyed wonderment.

Alessa looked down then, at the dark stain blossoming on the front of her skirt, and some part of her recognised it as the source of that distant pain. A ragged glass tooth emerged from her left thigh, a shard the size of her palm, and she let out a high, breathless laugh; how had she not realised?

Still, the pain seemed a long way away; even in her befuddled state Alessa knew she was in some kind of shock, and that this might be equally as dangerous as the window-shard buried in the meat of her thigh.

Breathe, she told herself.

Alessa exhaled, and the world finally came into sharp, awful focus.

That was when the crying began.

It was as if someone had suddenly turned up the volume. Behind her, in front of her, beneath her, a cacophony of voices pleading and crying and whimpering. Somewhere outside the carriage, one voice carried higher and louder than the rest, a howl so prolonged it seemed it might never end; an animal scream, torn from the throat of something horribly wounded. Alessa snatched her hand from the other woman's grasp, clutching at her own coat with trembling fingers. One bare foot scraped the ground. There was something wet beneath her toes. She drew her foot up, staring in dumb horror as one of the piles of upholstery lining the carriage began to move; slowly, hands and a face appearing in

11

the dark, smeared black with blood. They were people, she realised: people clutching desperately at her ankles as she walked over them, praying that she might save them.

She'd seen all this before, in snippets of grainy smartphone footage posted to YouTube and removed almost as quickly: the London Bridge tube bombings, five years ago. Two bombs in tandem, reducing the Northern Line tunnel to a scorched black mouth choked with rubble and dead bodies. The sour tang of charred electrics burnt in the back of her mouth. She swallowed it down. Two bombs. Alessa could not recall the exact moment of the explosion, but she knew there had only been one. So far.

"We need to get off the train," Alessa said. She didn't wait for the other woman's response. The doors either side of the carriage were jammed shut, windows blown out by the explosion; coronas of broken glass jutted from their steel frames. The door linking the carriages hung limp from its hinges. Alessa approached the empty space with trepidation.

The next carriage was pitch black, but the dark outlines of objects slumped on the floor were horribly visible. A wave of dizziness hit her like a punch to the gut. Her legs buckled suddenly beneath her. She grabbed the doorframe for support, bracing both hands against it. *Just breathe*, she told herself, squeezing her eyes shut. She drew in a deep, shuddering breath and tried not to think about the way the air tasted.

When she opened her eyes, the disembodied light of a mobile phone danced in the space to her left, down in the tunnel, a cold blue firefly in the black.

"Are you alone?" a voice called out.

"There's one other," Alessa said. "I think. There are...I think there are a lot of injured people in here." She hated how casual she sounded, as if the people in the aisle were items on an inventory. The enormity of it all hadn't struck her yet – that would come later, in the back of an ambulance, clinging to a grim-faced paramedic's hand just to feel the pulse of another living person. Despite the ache in her leg and the dust on her tongue it still felt as though all of this was nothing more substantial than an extraordinarily vivid hallucination.

There came the sound of two voices conferring, lost beneath the tinny ring in Alessa's ears. "It's safe to come down here, the power is out. Can you walk?" the first voice asked. Male, lightly accented – Polish, maybe, Alessa had never been good at placing accents. The blue-lit profile of a man's face came briefly into focus. His forehead was dark with blood.

"I think so," Alessa said. Cautiously, she clambered down, broken glass crunching beneath her bare feet. She barely felt it. The shard lodged in her leg shot a flare of pain up through the muscles of her thigh, twisting into the small of her back. Someone held out an arm and she took it, grateful for the stability.

"I'm going to check the carriage," a second voice said. "I can hear someone in there."

Alessa could too. A low keening, ghostly in the dark. "There was another woman," she told the man beside her, as he guided her down the tracks, away from the train. She didn't look back. She couldn't. "She was hurt, I…she wouldn't come with me." Guilt seized her like a sudden chill. "I should go back for her," she said, turning away. "I have first aid training. I should be helping."

"You're wounded," the man said, eyeing her with some scepticism. "It's no good for you to help anyone. You're bleeding."

"But..."

"That man, Gareth, he's a nurse. He'll help her."

"Are you staff?"

She heard him laugh, a bitter sound. "No. I haven't seen any staff. The emergency lights haven't even come on. Just us for now."

As they made their way to the back of the train, she saw others climbing down from the carriages. The damage wasn't quite as bad this far down, although that same rank, acrid smell seemed to permeate the air. It was colder here; Alessa was suddenly conscious of her bare foot, and the sting of the chill air against her lacerated skin.

A hundred questions swirled in the haze of her confusion. She opened her mouth to ask the man what had happened, but stopped short. How would he know? He was fumbling through the dark, same as her. And the probable answer was obvious. Terrorist attack. Wasn't it always?

"Where were you going?" It felt like a terribly inane question, but the agonised cries of the unseen wounded ricocheted inside her aching skull, and if she had to listen to it any longer she thought she might scream.

"Home." The lights were still on in the far carriages, illuminating the tunnel somewhat, and she could see him more clearly now. Tall, clean-shaven, profile like a boxer's; flat, broad nose and sloping Neanderthal forehead. He was dressed in a black jacket and a crisp white shirt, though the collar was soaked through with blood. His, or someone else's, Alessa wasn't certain. "I was working the late shift. I left twenty minutes early." He let out another sharp bark of laughter. "I have never left work early in my whole life. Maybe God is trying to tell me something."

"I was at a party." Alessa said. She was limping badly now, her head buzzing with the effort. She wanted more than anything just to lie down and rest. "I...I don't usually go to parties. I lost track of time. I should be back home already."

A small cluster of walking wounded had assembled at the end of the train. Further down the tunnel was Elephant and Castle station, where the train had been due to terminate. If help was coming, it was likely coming from that direction. Like her, the other people were in various states of injury. One woman had her arm wrapped in a blue silk scarf; blood had already seeped through the fabric, staining it dark and glossy. Another sat on the tracks, legs drawn to her chest, trembling violently; what little Alessa could see of her face was terribly swollen, the tissue raw and shining in the glow of the man's mobile phone.

"Nobody's coming," said an elderly man, leaning heavily on the wall. His torn trousers hung like limp streamers around his calves.

"They will." A young man with a ponytail clutching a cello case, once white but smeared now with substances Alessa didn't want to think about. "They have to."

"I should go back," Alessa said, turning to the man who'd walked her down. "I can help."

The man shook his head. "You stay," he said. "You can't even stand up properly."

He was right. Alessa's leg was a stiff, useless thing, driving daggers up into her spine each time she took a step. There were major arteries down there, and the damp stickiness of her skin made her wonder exactly what had been damaged.

"There's a light." The man slid his mobile into his pocket, shutting off the ambient glow. Alessa squinted off into the tunnel. Somewhere further down, there was a pinprick of yellowish light, disembodied in the black. A torch, perhaps. It seemed a very long way off, but the dark was deceptive.

"Could be help arriving," the man said. "I'm going down to meet them. Will you be okay here, just for a few minutes?"

Alessa wasn't certain if he was addressing her. She wasn't certain of anything much. She gave a vague nod. "We'll be fine," she said. It seemed to be all the assurance the man needed, because he set off immediately. The sound of his feet crunching on the gravel grew fainter, his silhouette eventually fading seamlessly into the shadows.

The woman with the burnt face began to cry, then, and Alessa struggled to crouch beside her. She touched a hand to the woman's wrist, feeling the reassuring solidity of her skin, her bones. "What's your name?" Alessa asked.

"Deborah." Her mouth strained to form the syllables, skin pulled tight across her teeth. Alessa regretted asking her. She squeezed the woman's shoulder and felt her answer, a trembling hand seeking Alessa's own.

"Okay, Deborah," Alessa said gently, lacing their fingers together tightly. "We're safe now. You're going to be fine." It was a lie; even in the dark the damage to her skin was obvious, and the last thing Deborah was going to be, when she got out of here and saw the raw mess of her face, was fine.

There came a shout from behind them. Alessa turned, and raised a hand to her eyes as a small army of bright torches came out of the gloom. "Everyone okay down there?" someone shouted.

"Some of us are hurt," the silk scarf woman replied. She'd joined Alessa in the middle of the tracks. The torch-bearers approached, bringing with them more walking wounded – ghastly, soot-smeared people shambling like zombies. Some supported others, moving in slow tandem, talking amongst themselves in low voices.

One woman had a scarf tied tight around a sleeve which seemed horribly empty below the elbow.

"Ambulances are on their way. How many of you are there?" A torch swept over them, so obtrusively bright it made Alessa's eyes water.

"Five," the silk scarf woman said.

"Six," Alessa corrected. "There was another man. He saw someone with a torch coming this way. He went up to Elephant and Castle to meet them."

"Nobody's coming from Elephant and Castle, love," said the man holding the torch. "Not that I've heard of. The train's closer to Lambeth North. So, five here and a sixth further down. Don't go anywhere. Paramedics are on their way, okay?"

Two other men in hi-vis vests corralled the new group of walking wounded forward, forming a large, hushed mass of people too shocked and afraid to look one another properly in the eye. Alessa stroked the burnt woman's shoulder and stared up at the other survivors. A tall, bearded man whose soot-stained turban had begun to unravel; another beside him braced against the sloping tunnel wall, staring with unblinking eyes at the back of the train. "What happened?" someone asked. "Was it a bomb?"

"Had to be," another woman replied. She was haggard-looking but seemed otherwise unhurt, crouching over a barely-conscious man stretched out on the tracks. "Did you see how bad it was at the front?"

Deborah's sobs were loud in Alessa's ears as she peered down into the far reaches of the tunnel. The shadows seemed to ebb before her eyes, shifting like black water in an ocean abyss, but perhaps that was only the blood loss; everything seemed a little indistinct, a little fuzzy at the edges. There was no sign of the man, though; it was as though he'd never been there at all. He'll come back, Alessa thought. Once he realises nobody's coming that way. He'll come back and find us.

Later – after weeping uncontrollably in the back of an ambulance, prompting a shot of mild sedative, after the wound in her leg had been cleaned and assessed and stitched neatly up, after her sister came to see her, all red eyes and streaming nose, and insisted Alessa stay with her because she couldn't possibly be alone tonight, not after this – only then, laying sleepless in her sister's foldout bed, did Alessa realise that the man never had come back.

*

"We can stop there, if you like."

Alessa hadn't realised she'd been crying until the counsellor passed her a box of Kleenex. She tugged a handful of tissues, pressing them to her eyes. They came back black with smudged mascara. Makeup had been a mistake.

"I appreciate how hard this must be for you," Moira said. It seemed to Alessa that Moira always tried very hard to appear as though she *understood* how Alessa felt. She would sit there with her immaculate blonde bob and neatly-applied pink lipstick, tasteful jewellery and heels just a little too high to be practical, nodding intently as Alessa talked about finding herself surrounded by horrifically wounded human beings like she had any idea what that might feel like.

A framed portrait of Moira's three children sat proudly on the desk, each child dressed in improbably clean white clothing. Her office was filled with 'quirky' trinkets – a set of ceramic jars shaped like cupcakes, cushions printed with artsy black-and-white French bulldogs. Moira's idea of a traumatic experience was probably scrubbing red wine stains out of her cream carpet.

"I'm not sure that you do," Alessa said, balling up the black-smeared tissue in her hands. She knew she was being unfair; Moira's concern was probably genuine, but Alessa found it hard to trust a person so emphatically professing empathy where none could truly exist.

Moira smiled. "Try to explain it to me," she said, folding her hands neatly in her lap.

Alessa chewed the inside of her cheek. What was the proper way to express to someone that, a month on from the explosion, the mere thought of setting foot on a tube train made her chest constrict so tightly she could barely breathe? That although she had seen and heard things no person should ever have to witness, it wasn't Deborah's pink, churned flesh or the glass embedded in a woman's face or even the hand clutching desperately at her discarded shoe that she saw when she closed her eyes at night?

They'd all shown up at some time or another, these visions, stuttering like an old showreel. But almost every night of Alessa's life since the bomb, she dreamed of the man who'd disappeared. Always seen in profile, that flat boxer's nose and the ribbons of blood streaming from his scalp. She tried, mute and frustrated, to call out to him: to tell him not to go, that help was coming from the other direction. Every time, he walked off alone into the shifting darkness, towards that pinprick of torchlight. Not once did he return.

She stared up at Moira. Her head was tilted ever so slightly to one side, awaiting Alessa's answer like a patient dog.

"I haven't been sleeping very well," Alessa said, finally.

"Don't the tablets help?"

They did, a little too well. The problem wasn't *getting* to sleep; Alessa seemed to exist in a permanent state of exhaustion, nodding off at the most inopportune moments. The problem was what happened when she fell asleep. The problem was the dreams, and the man who never came back.

"Not really," Alessa said.

"I'm reluctant to give you anything stronger," Moira said, frowning at Alessa's notes. "Have you considered any alternative therapies? I can put you in touch with a wonderful yoga instructor. Proper relaxation techniques can do wonders for insomnia."

Alessa forced a smile. "That would be good, thank you," she said, hoping she sounded more enthusiastic than she felt. Suddenly, she was desperate to get out of this room, to breathe clean air. "Maybe you could email me the details," she said, but Moira had already unearthed a leaflet. Moira had leaflets for just about everything.

"I think you're making very good progress, Alessa," Moira said, watching Alessa fold the leaflet in half without even glancing at it. "We both knew this was going to be a long, hard process, but you're doing exceptionally well. I'm glad you were able to talk about what happened. It's important to be able to face these things, especially if you're called to speak at the inquest."

"Very important, yes," Alessa said, nodding. That was the key to surviving these sessions, she'd learned; nodding in the right places and agreeing with the counsellor, even if you thought they were talking total nonsense.

Perhaps there were better counsellors out there, ones who knew how best to approach the open wound of post-traumatic stress, but Moira Monaghan was not one of those counsellors. She was hopelessly out of her depth, well-meaning but largely ineffectual. It wasn't her fault; she hadn't had the training, had been drafted in at the last minute to cope with the sudden swell of trauma patients, and Alessa sometimes sensed that Moira was as uncomfortable with the arrangement as she was.

Alessa's pleas to be transferred had gone largely unheard – lost, perhaps, in the great paperwork vortex of the NHS. She was lucky to have access to a counsellor at all, her sister told her. There were people out there who'd been on the waiting list for far longer.

Out in the car-park, the gloom of the office gave way to lukewarm spring sunshine. Alessa shielded her eyes with one hand. The Shard was a spire of white glass, painfully bright; the lumpen protrusion of Guy's Tower shielded the worst of the glare. It was a monstrously ugly building. When she was a child, and the skyline hadn't been half as cluttered, the hospital tower had resembled some kind of giant animal, complete with silver cylinder ears. Nestled now among bright glass and polished steel it seemed a sad old thing, diminished and decaying like so much of the London she recalled from her childhood.

Ahead stood the railway arch, and beneath it London Bridge station. Perhaps it was a sign of progress that the familiar red-and-blue underground symbol no longer sent her heart into immediate spasm. Perhaps Moira had been good for something. But if she thought too hard about the escalators trundling down into the depths, or the platforms flanked by wide, black tunnel-mouths the breath would stick in her chest, and a sick, sour weight would form in her gut. Moira called it a 'panic spiral'. It seemed as accurate a description as any; a dizzying descent into nausea, breathlessness so intense the world around her seemed to disappear entirely. And suddenly she would find herself back there on the tracks, holding

Deborah's hand, the stink of burnt flesh hot in her nostrils.

Alessa studiously avoided the station, walking down the quieter back roads. It was a longer route, but it wasn't like she had much else to do. Even before the bomb it had been months since she'd had anything like a regular job. She'd thought about reapplying to the agencies, sending her CV to the local schools. It'd be good for her to restore some semblance of normality. To be a part of the world again.

She reached the bus stop just as the bus was pulling in. It was late April but the heaters were still on, and the air inside the bus felt unpleasantly damp, a miasma of sweat and condensation. She sat beside a window, turning her face up to the scant breeze trickling in.

Alessa had never liked buses much. They moved ponderously, trundling through traffic and pausing at red lights. Perhaps it was some unconscious snobbery but buses seemed like mobile havens for strange behaviour. People *talked* on the bus, to one another and their phones and sometimes to complete strangers. She'd always appreciated the comparative quiet of the Tube, where eye contact was forbidden, and people spoke in hushed tones, if at all.

And there she was again, thinking of the Underground as though she'd ever be able to set foot on it again without panicking. Remembering the sardine-tin crush of commuter bodies made her acutely aware of her own heart, and the way it beat just a little too hard against her ribcage. *'This is the start of your panic-spiral,'* she heard Moira say. She closed her eyes, drew in a deep breath and, in her head, began naming the bones: *Occipital, parietal, frontal, temporal, sphenoid...*

It had seemed ridiculous when Moira had first proposed it. She'd suggested counting backwards from fifty, or reciting something simple – the Lord's Prayer, perhaps. (Alessa had rejected that one outright, not least because her joyless Protestant mother might have approved). Later, when the panic attacks wouldn't stop coming and Alessa was desperate enough to try anything, it'd been her sister Shannon – paediatric nurse and know-it-all - who had suggested she memorise the individual bones of the human body. It was a game they'd played as girls, asserting intellectual superiority through memorising trivia – an ultra-competitive 'bet-you-can't' which had endured into adulthood.

...ethmoid, nasal, maxillae, lacrimal...

Alessa cracked open an eye. Nobody was watching her. Outside, the bus eased through the traffic, slipping beneath the railway bridge onto Bermondsey Street. The bright spring sunshine gave way temporarily to dank gloom.

...zygomatic, palatine...

Three men in grubby overalls got on, moving upstairs in a close-knit cluster. A harried-looking woman struggled on board with a pram piled high with Tesco bags, followed closely by a thin man with skin the colour of spoiled milk, toothpick arms protruding from a baggy Motorhead t-shirt. He smelled of unwashed skin and worn leather, and a faint undertone of day-old skunk. She turned her face to the window, hoping the breeze might help dilute the odour.

In the window, a face stared back.

Alessa's limbs jolted sharply. Her heart seemed to seize for a few seconds, squeezing like a clenched fist in her chest. An empty black face save for pale grey pinhole eyes, staring up at her, meeting her wide-eyed gaze with utter impunity. A smudged charcoal sketch of something vaguely humanoid, limbs long and spider-thin. It sat there for a moment, boneless in the seat beside her; it blinked languidly, lids like shutters sliding over those hard grey eyes. *A shadow*, she thought, swallowing down the bilious panic burning at her throat. *Just a shadow.* She held her breath as she turned to look at the seat beside her.

It was empty. Nothing there but worn upholstery. One hand clutched unconsciously at her throat, pulse rapid beneath her fingers. The thin man across the aisle side-eyed Alessa and shuffled further along in his seat, staring pointedly at his mobile.

By the time she found the courage to look back to the window, the bus had veered out into the sunlit street once more, and the shadow – if it had ever been there at all – was gone.

She wanted to feel stupid. Alessa Spiteri, twenty-seven years old and literally jumping at shadows. But all she felt was a strange pressure on her chest, like strong hands pushing down, and she found herself hurriedly leaving her seat, thumb pressing repeatedly on the bell as she slipped into the aisle.

At the next stop the doors slid open with a tired hiss; she scrambled onto the pavement, gulping in diesel fumes like she might never get to breathe again. As the bus pulled off she saw a woman and her little girl settling into the seat where the shadow had been, blissfully unaware that anything strange had ever happened.

She stood in the sunlight, propped woozily against the bus shelter. Her heart beat with the staccato haste of a frightened animal.

"Are you unwell?"

Alessa turned sharply, startling the little Asian woman who'd questioned her. She had pebbly little glasses and long a black braid shot through with bright streaks of white. She approached Alessa with slow caution. "You don't look very well," the woman said. "You should sit down."

"No," Alessa said. There were others at the bus stop and every one of them was gawking at her, though some at least had the courtesy to pretend they weren't. She *did* feel stupid then; her fingers ached as she peeled her hands from the frame of the bus shelter. "No, thank you. I'm okay now. I'm fine."

The look on the woman's face suggested Alessa did not look fine, but she didn't attempt to stop Alessa scurrying away from the bus stop, cheeks flushed in embarrassment, her pulse still thundering in her throat.

TWO

Alessa hadn't been far from home but she backtracked all the same, heading for her sister's flat in Blackfriars. She wound through backstreets she knew with intimate familiarity, past off-licences and launderettes and trees frothing with pale pink blossom, plastic bags caught and billowing in their boughs. The streets were bathed in sunshine and shadows were few and far between, but Alessa found herself studiously avoiding windows, gaze fixed only on the distance ahead.

Shadow-ghosts in the bus window. "Straight out of the bloody Twilight Zone," she muttered to herself. "Shannon's going to laugh herself sick."

Alessa huddled deep into her jacket as she walked. Despite the clear blue sky and bright, high sun, the air still smelled faintly of winter; a cold, pervasive dampness, lingering even as the dew dried from the grass. She felt like she'd been in hibernation for a long time; all those numb hours on the sofa, awakening as if from a dream only to realise she'd been staring at the wall for the better part of three hours. She felt as though she was only barely a part of the world sometimes, existing on some strange margin inhabited by the anxious and the scared and the mad. Her hair hung in tangles, her skin sallow. Sometimes, she'd catch herself in a mirror, staring in horror at the smudges beneath her eyes, deep as bruises, and wonder just how she'd let herself slip so badly.

It was a sentiment Shannon echoed when she opened the door, eyes widening first in surprise, then in mild horror. "Wow, what underpass did you wake up in?" she asked, pulling momentarily away from the phone she was holding. Alessa squeezed past her into the narrow hallway, made narrower still by the abundance of mismatched artwork lining the walls: a replica canvas of Van Gogh's Starry Night sat egregiously beside a gaudy Sex Pistols poster Shannon had bought specifically to irritate their mother.

"Thanks."

"Be right with you. Got mum on the phone." Offhanded, but Alessa caught the roll of her eyes as she sidled off into the kitchen.

Alessa went into the living room and put her coat and bag on the dining table - a small square of glass which might seat two at a push. She sat in the armchair, taking care to turn her back to the window. The flat was only just big enough to accommodate people, let alone furniture, and the communal areas were usually in want of a good deep clean, but Shannon always said the river view made up for everything else.

Shannon came in from the kitchen with a bottle of white wine and two glasses. "I can't…" Alessa began, but the glass appeared in her hand, and Shannon poured until it threatened to overflow.

"You can," Shannon replied, pouring herself an equally voluminous glass. "You will. Because I sure as hell need a drink after speaking to mum, and you look like you could do with one too."

Alessa wriggled forward in her chair, placing the glass on the coffee table. "You're not supposed to mix antidepressants and alcohol."

Shannon made a face. "We both know you're not taking the antidepressants," she said. "It's good wine, and expensive, and

I'm not going to let you waste it, so just bloody drink it." She led by example, draining half her glass in one go. She wiped her mouth with the back of her hand. "Jesus, she's hard work."

"What did she want?" The wine tasted pleasantly dry, clearing some of the fog from her brain. Shannon looked utterly frazzled, barely recovered from the night shift; her blonde hair was scraped back into a stringy ponytail, her face scrubbed and shiny.

"Oh, she thinks she's dying. Again." A wave of the hand. "She's been feeling faint. She wanted me to check her blood pressure. It *has* been a little high lately, but that's because she drinks about thirty cups of coffee a day. I told her to cut down on the caffeine and try eating proper food for once. Have you seen the size of her?" Shannon shook her head and refilled her glass. "She's just skin, bone and dust at this point. No wonder she's been feeling faint. I'd send her for bloods, but I'm not sure she's got any."

Alessa let out a little snort of laughter. "You're cruel."

"She looks *ancient*," Shannon said, with something approaching horror. "Jesus, I hope I take after dad. He didn't look like a dried-out old mummy at sixty."

"He was seventeen stone. How many fat mummies have you ever seen?" In their wedding pictures her parents had appeared comically mismatched – Eleanor, small and dainty as the iced flowers on their wedding-cake, and Marco, six foot one and built like a barrel, big and round and solid. In the last few months of his life his weight had plummeted with alarming speed, revealing the surprisingly delicate bones of him beneath like a frame upon which her father had been built, layer by layer. The first thing the cancer had robbed him of was his appetite. That had always seemed especially cruel to Alessa. Food had been her father's greatest joy in life, surpassed only by his daughters.

Alessa looked down at her own layer of flab spilling over the waistband of her jeans – diminished since the bomb, because constant gut-wrenching anxiety and food had proven to be largely incompatible, but persistent all the same.

Shannon smiled, a little sadly. "But anyway. Never mind mum. Why are you here?"

Right up until Shannon opened the front door, she'd been ready to tell her everything: the nightmares about the disappearing man, and the thing in the window, the black shadow staring intently at her with pale pinprick eyes. Shannon would listen, and she would not laugh, not really; she was a paediatric nurse, it was her job to entertain all manner of fears and phobias and concerns, even monsters under the bed. But she wouldn't understand it. How could she?

I saw a monster in the window and I'm fixated on a man I never even saw properly, Alessa thought, taking a gulp of wine for courage. *How do I expect anyone to understand a thing like that?*

"I had a panic attack on the bus," Alessa said. "It's not the first time it's happened, but this was different to anything I've experienced before. The bus went under a bridge, and it was dark, and - well, this is going to sound mental, but I think I sort of…hallucinated."

"Hallucinated?" Shannon frowned. "How do you mean? Has it happened before?"

"Well, I mean, it wasn't a hallucination *exactly*," Alessa backtracked, aware of the suspicion in Shannon's eyes. "It was…I was fine. Even when the bus went under the bridge, I was fine. But then I looked at the window, and…" She stopped short. The words remained stuck stubbornly to the roof her mouth: *I saw a monster. It stared at me, and then it disappeared.* "I don't know," Alessa finished lamely. She pressed her fingers to her forehead; her brain had begun to throb. It must have been the wine. "I don't know what it was. Shadows playing tricks on my eyes, I suppose. I just panicked. I had to get off the bus before my head exploded." She exhaled. It sounded like a sigh. "Maybe I'm going mad."

She felt Shannon's hand on her shoulder. Somehow, she'd crossed the room and perched on the arm of the chair without Alessa noticing. "You're being hard on yourself," she said. In the full light of the window she looked tired; the skin beneath her eyes was thin and papery, revealing a delta of blue-green veins. "You expect too much, too soon. I know how much you want to get back to work, but you need to give yourself time. Why don't you mention it to Moira at your next session?"

"Moira's full of shit," Alessa said.

"Oh, whatever." Shannon's smug, lopsided smirk hadn't changed since childhood. "You're not letting her *help* you, that's the problem. She's not offering you easy answers and you can't stand it, so you've decided she's no good to you. You can't go through life assuming you can do everything by yourself. That's always been your problem. That's why you're still having trouble coping."

Alessa's hackles rose instinctively, but Shannon had hit close to the mark. She rubbed absently at her arms, shifted uncomfortably in her seat.

"Speaking of Moira," Shannon said. "There's a trauma support group who meet every couple of weeks at the hospital. It was set up by survivors of the London Bridge bombing. They've got a meeting tomorrow afternoon sometime. You're always saying how Moira doesn't understand what you went through, and I get that, but these people shared your experiences. They saw the things you did. I think it would be good for you, talking with people who get it."

"I'll think about it," Alessa said, though the mere thought of it made her itch somewhere deep beneath the skin; it was too much like exposure, a display of emotional nakedness in front of complete strangers.

"You're tough, Alessa. I know you're not going to let something like this beat you. Christ, I remember when you were twelve and you broke your ankle…It was at the adventure playground on Harper Road, do you remember it? The bone was practically sticking out of your foot and you refused to go to the hospital because it would ruin your birthday?"

Alessa let out a snort of laughter. "How would you even remember that? You were what, eight? Dad promised I could have another birthday party if I went with him to A&E." She lifted her glass to her lips. Somehow, it was full again. She drank deep, savouring the crisp taste. "I never did get another party."

"He made all kinds of promises," Shannon said, a little wistful. "He used to say stuff without ever really thinking about how realistic it was. That's why mum used to shoot him down. We thought she was such a killjoy, but somebody had to do it. Remember when he promised us we could have chickens in the garden? We lived in a council flat, for god's sake, the garden was the size of a wheelie bin."

Alessa placed her empty glass back on the coffee table. Her body felt a little slower than normal, as if she were half asleep, and a pleasant warmth had seeped deep into her muscles. "I miss him," she said. "I haven't stopped missing him. Is that strange? I keep thinking I should be used to it by now, but there's a part of me that expects to hear his voice when I pick up the phone. And I'm always disappointed when I hear mum's instead. God, what a horrible thing to say." She stared down at her hands; broad fingers like her father's, the same blunt, chewed nails. "I keep thinking. If he were here I'd be coping so much better with all of this. He always knew what to tell me. He always made me feel safe. Why am I even saying this?"

"In vino, veritas," Shannon said, with a thin smile. "I miss him too, Ali. I know you two were closer, but..." She trailed off, looking momentarily thoughtful. Then, without a word, she got up and headed into the kitchen. When she came back she was holding another bottle of white wine in one hand, and a family pack of Monster Munch in the other.

"It's Asda's own," she said, by way of apology. "But wine is wine, isn't it? Here, give me your glass." She filled them both back up. Alessa could smell this wine from a distance, sharp and acid. Shannon handed Alessa her glass back and lifted her own. "To dad," she declared. "Wherever you are. I hope every night is steak night, and there's red wine on tap, and more books than you can ever hope to read."

"To dad," Alessa said. Her throat suddenly felt very full. The world blurred, as if seen through a rain-wet window, and she looked down into her wine, blinking furiously.

"Oh Ali." She heard Shannon rise from her seat, the creak of leather as she shifted her slight weight. And then her sister's arms were around her, and she couldn't hold the tears back any more. She had cried so hard and for so long when her dad died that, at his funeral, hers had been the only dry eyes in the church. She'd simply run out. The sadness had grown inside of her, festering like an abscess, and it seemed she might never be rid of it; a deep, dull pain radiating out as though from the very marrow of her bones. It was not healthy, she knew, to bottle up grief but it hadn't been a choice. She had done all the crying at his bedside, and her body had deemed it enough.

She hadn't cried again until after the bomb.

"Poor Ali," Shannon said. "You've been through so much these last few months." She smelled warm, reassuring; Dove soap and white wine and the faint salt tang of unwashed hair.

"I've got no right to feel this way," Alessa said. Her voice sounded quiet in the protective cocoon of Shannon's arms. "I wasn't badly hurt. I didn't lose anyone. I was just *there*."

"Don't be an idiot." Shannon held her at arm's length, mouth stern. "Other people suffered worse that day, yes. But that doesn't diminish your own grief. You're

45

allowed to hurt, Alessa. Your feelings are just as important as theirs."

"You sound like Moira." Alessa scrubbed at her eyes with the heel of her palm. Her nose felt plugged with mucus.

Shannon smiled. "I've got your back. You know that. And you can always talk to me about things, all right?"

She thought of ink-black limbs, long and bone-thin, of pale staring eyes.

"I know," Alessa said.

*

Shannon was highly skilled in the art of distraction. It was practically a requirement in her field of work, she said; keeping young patients occupied while they had a cannula fitted, playing repetitive games with them to take their minds off their illness. Alessa let herself be distracted. They finished the wine in front of the TV; the presence of it was strangely soothing, filling Alessa's brain with meaningless noise and colour until her anxiety seemed to recede, a tide slowly going out until it was a mere line on the horizon.

Before long, Shannon was sound asleep on the sofa and Alessa remained stubbornly awake, wrapped in a blanket and listening to her sister snore in the grey gloom. She kept thinking about what she'd seen in the bus window, and the more she considered it, the more certain she was that she must have imagined it in her panic.

Alessa was not quite drunk – not like Shannon – but the wine had made her bold. She got up quietly from the sofa, blanket draped over her shoulders. The laminate was cold beneath her bare feet. She padded across the room, over to the window where the curtains hung, dark and heavy. She wouldn't see anything, she told herself. There was nothing *to* see. Malevolent shadow-presences were not real.

Slowly, and with great caution, she parted the curtains.

The lights lining the Thames glowed gold, the night sky the murky purple of a fresh bruise. High up, the bright light of a passing plane cut through the scudding clouds like a torch in the dark. The river was stained pink and blue as the neon colours of the city bled out into the high tide.

Something quick and dark moved in the corner of her eye. Her heart gave a momentary leap, but the shape quickly resolved itself into the narrow silhouette of a fox scurrying along the embankment, slinking from shadow to shadow.

Alessa looked up. There was her reflection, a pale ghost in the glass. The only ghastly thing staring out from the window was herself: puffy and hollow-eyed, surrounded by a wild halo of dark hair. Tipsy laughter bubbled up in her chest and she clamped her teeth hard to keep it there. What she'd seen on the bus had been a trick of the light, her anxiety taking control and warping the mundane into the horrific. There was a great sense of relief, a draining of pent-up adrenaline like a lanced abscess.

Behind her, Shannon muttered something in her sleep. Alessa let the curtains slip closed, padding back to the sofa in the dark. Quietly, she gathered up her coat and bag. The display on her phone read 10.43pm. She could stay here if she wanted, but sleep was a distant promise and her newly restless limbs wanted to walk, to run, to move. She would go home, and tomorrow she would get up early, start clearing up the accumulated clutter and mess that had piled up like a landslide in the days when getting out of bed had seemed an insurmountable challenge.

Alessa scrawled a note for Shannon on the back of an envelope – *thanks for the wine & chat, hope your head isn't too sore in the morning! Love ya A x* – and used her spare key to lock the door behind her.

*

In the absence of spring sunshine the air was sharp and chilly, and strangely sobering. Alessa buried her nose in the fur collar of her parka, breathing warmth into the confined space beneath. The streets around Shannon's flat were quiet. The occasional car passed by, headlights bright, wheels hissing on tarmac. She passed a housing estate, looking steadily past the cluster of hoodies stood at the entrance like sentinels, their faces sallow in the glare of the streetlights. They followed her progress with their eyes.

Her mouth was as fuzzy as her head. As she walked, some of the heaviness in her limbs began to subside. Shannon might have been younger, but Alessa had inherited their father's tolerance for alcohol. Still, when she turned into a series of side streets and realised she was no longer certain where she was, she instinctively blamed it on the wine. She'd walked this route so many times it was ingrained into her memory, a map scrawled on the inside of her skull, but here she was, standing in the mouth of a narrow street she was certain she'd never walked down before. She frowned, turning a circle in search of a sign. Loman Street. Offices on the right, a long, windowless building on the left. Somewhere along the way she'd taken a wrong turn.

The mosquito whine of a building alarm sounded from somewhere nearby. She heard the low thrum of traffic ahead; a main road, still busy even at this hour. It would be easy enough to get her bearings there. She set off, suddenly aware of how dark it was down here, how few of the street lights seemed to be functional. The sour smell of overripe binbags drifted in on the wind. The shrill sound of the alarm seemed to carry a long way in the quiet. Her shadow waxed and waned as she passed between the lights, limbs stretched, form distorted. Just like…

No. She shoved her hands in her pockets. *It wasn't real. I proved that.*

Behind her, close by, something skittered out into the road.

A fox, she told herself, though she felt her pace quicken, her muscles tightening. *Lots of foxes around here.* The sound came again, closer still, and it seemed that there were eyes on her, tracking her frantic motion; her fingers closed around the keys in her pocket, slipping them between her knuckles.

Occipital, parietal...

She was tipsy and alone, and a woman walking solo on a dark, isolated street was an easy target. Her screams would be lost beneath the wail of the alarm. Nobody would come for her. Nobody would know she was here.

Frontal, temporal, sphenoid...

She sucked in a deep breath and peered over her shoulder.

Something long and thin retreated into the shadows.

Alessa ran. Her heart was alive in her chest, struggling against her ribcage. She would not look back. She sprinted the last fifty metres, her ragged breath loud in her own ears. She turned out onto the main road and collided heavily with a man coming the other way.

"Careful, love," the man said, taking a step back. "Watch where you're going."

There was life out here, and lights and motion but her nerves were sparking at random and the breath didn't quite seem to be reaching her lungs. Wide-eyed, she nodded a frantic apology, but the man was already on his way. Maybe he'd smelled the wine on her, taken her for a lush. Alessa stared out at the passing traffic. She knew this road, and she knew how to get back home from here. The lights were bright, the road still busy. She would be safe now.

It took all of her courage to look back into the mouth of Loman Street.

There was nothing. Bathed in an orange-gold glow, the street seemed no more sinister than any other street. There were a hundred things which might have made the noise she'd heard, and only a fraction of them were dangerous. Alessa's spine slackened a little, a sigh escaping her lungs. Why was her imagination suddenly so intent on burning holes in her sanity? And why did she keep falling for it?

She kept to the main roads the rest of the way.

*

Not until she was safely inside her own flat, door locked and latched behind her, did she truly allow herself to relax. The flat smelled warm and stale, of old food crusted on the hob and piles of unwashed clothes. It smelled safe.

She moved through the small space, flicking all the lights on so as to banish every shadow, every dark corner. She had never felt unsafe in her own home, not even after the bomb; she was not about to entertain the possibility now.

She picked up the least grubby glass from the sideboard, rinsed it under the tap and poured a glass of water. She hadn't realised quite how parched her throat was. She gulped it down in one go, the coldness of it tracing a path down her gullet. Her heart still fluttered unpleasantly in her chest, the dregs of her fear persistent as a bad headache.

Alessa went into the bedroom, leaving the kitchen light on behind her. Her sheets were in the same crumpled disarray she'd left them in this morning, the floor covered in a layer of discarded clothing. A leaning tower of half-read books rose haphazard from the nightstand. She peeled off her jacket and kicked off her shoes. She paused. Across the room, above the bed, the curtains were wide open. She was on the third floor, but her flat overlooked another block; she could see them, and she was reasonably sure they could see her. Alessa waded through clothing across to the other side of the room, one hand tugging at the button of her jeans, the other reaching for the curtain.

Outside, down in the car park, something moved.

She peered out. The car park was poorly lit, shadows merging with shadows in the light of a single, solitary lamppost. And something was moving there, a shape on the very edge of the darkness, undulating like the tail of a large animal.

A bolus of panic rose in her throat.

It lurked there a moment, barely visible but *there*, and when it finally came into the light – tentative, as if it might burn – she knew what it was. An oil-smear of a creature; the awful distortion of something almost human, crawling slowly on four long matchstick limbs. A narrow, elongated head bobbed limp on a thin neck. Pale eyes flickered open like newly-lit flames.

It looked up.

It saw her, and she looked back; she wanted to look away but she met its gaze, stared hard and unblinking. She had to know it was real, not a shadow or a trick of the light but something physical.

The skin of it peeled back, the space below the eyes opening like a shutter to reveal a gleaming lamprey mouth: a perfect circle of bright, needle-sharp teeth.

The books clattered to the floor as she swung her arms up, yanking both curtains shut.

Her hands gripped the curtains, holding them together; if she couldn't see it, it couldn't harm her. It was ridiculous logic, a child's logic, but she clung to it with the desperation of a drowning man. The front door was locked, all the windows shut. If she tried not to think, she could almost pretend that there was no car-park outside, no grinning shadow-thing standing just beyond the glow of the streetlight. She crossed back over and closed the bedroom door, pushing the plastic wedge as firmly beneath as it would go.

Alessa shucked off the rest of her clothes and crawled into her bed. She flipped both table lamps on, bathing the room in light. For weeks after the bomb she hadn't been able to sleep in the dark, afraid that she might wake up back in the tunnels. And here she was again, swaddled in blankets as though they might keep all the evils of the world away, afraid of the dark and what might lurk inside.

THREE

In the pale light of morning, after only a few hours of fitful, fearful sleep, two things were clear to Alessa. The first was that what she had seen last night had felt very real. Every instinct she possessed told her this was a sign of impending insanity, but she had *felt* its gaze worming beneath her skin, settling there like something malignant.

The second was that the trauma support group no longer sounded like a terrible idea.

Maybe this wasn't an unusual phenomenon. Maybe stress-induced hallucinations were common after a traumatic event. And maybe it would help, talking all of it through with people who'd been there, who'd emerged from the other side intact, if a little scarred. If it meant finding some small peace of mind then it had to be worth trying.

But talking about what she'd seen wasn't an option. Revealing something so clearly divorced from reality was surely a recipe for enforced convalescence. Perhaps they'd put her on antipsychotics, monitor her carefully to ensure she was taking them. Perhaps they'd lock her away. They'd never let her near a school again, not when the agencies found out about her 'issues'. *They're not real*, she told herself, as though strange, frightening visions were infinitely more comforting than real monsters. *None of this is real. You're stressed and upset. You need help.*

She dug her laptop out from beneath a mound of old magazines. A quick Google search revealed the 'Healing Hearts Group', organised by a woman named Teresa Osterman who, the website explained, had lost an eye in the London Bridge bombings five years previous. She, along with a couple of other survivors, had organised the group as a sort of informal catharsis, a meeting of people who'd experienced the same horrors and were struggling to readjust to the world in the wake of it all.

The mere thought of dealing with other human beings filled her with a bone-deep exhaustion. Not even in the bright, shadowless light of morning did she want to open the curtains and acknowledge the world beyond. She dozed fitfully on the sofa, pulled constantly from the precipice of deep sleep by the fear of what she might dream of. Distantly, she was aware that she was regressing to the same behaviours she'd adopted after the bomb.

In the early afternoon she forced herself to leave the house, taking a slow walk up through Southwark to St Thomas'. It was a large and sprawling hospital, spread out over several buildings, their architecture discordant. Sunlight bounced off the windows, reflecting back a piecemeal image of County Hall against a cloud-spattered blue sky.

There had been frost on the ground in November, when she was last here. She remembered carving patterns in the ice with the toe of her boot, occasionally pausing to stare up at the window her father lay behind. His bed had boasted a spectacular view of Westminster Bridge and the London Eye revolving slowly against the grey sky. He had never been awake for long enough to enjoy it. The faint sound of Gipsy Kings filtered out from the headphones pressed against his ears – the ones Shannon had insisted they put there, because even in his unconsciousness she was sure he would be able to hear it.

He'd smelled of fever-sweat and antiseptic; the bones of his chest were visible in the gap of his hospital gown, skin strung paper-thin from rib to rib, a sallow canopy. She would spend hours at his bedside staring out of the windows, listening to the slow, persistent rhythm of the heart monitor, aware that at any moment, it could all come to an end. Praying that it would. And her father had lain there, tubes and wires protruding like pale tentacles, oblivious to the view, to the world, to everything but still, silent darkness.

Alessa arrived ten minutes late. Upstairs, the group had already gathered and were talking when she approached, sidling quietly up to the open door. She peered through the gap. There were more people than she'd imagined there might be. The chairs were arranged in a haphazard circle; a man in a navy cable-knit jumper appeared to be the focal point. He had an unflattering ginger beard and a clipboard. An NHS badge on a lanyard around his neck suggested he worked at St Thomas' in some capacity.

"I still have trouble sleeping," a woman was saying. The puckered red outline of a recent scar peeked out from the deep V of her shirt, dissonant against her dark skin. Alessa didn't recognise her. "I manage to drop off but every little thing seems to wake me up again. My next-door neighbour works night shifts, and when she starts her car up…I *know* it's going to happen every night, but it still scares the life out of me."

Beside her sat a man with horrendous scarring to the left side of his face; bleached ridges of flesh puckered outwards, fading into a patchy hairline. It was an old wound. The London Bridge bombings had been far more severe than the Elephant and Castle incident; sixteen dead and scores injured, many of them disabled for life. A multitude of terrorist organisations had tried to claim responsibility. But nobody had come forward to claim the Elephant and Castle bombing for their own. The police, it was rumoured, were at a loose end to explain who'd been responsible.

Alessa slipped away from the door, pressing her back flat against the wall. There were too many people in there. People who were already familiar with one another, familiar with the intimacy of this process. She imagined their eyes trained upon her as she spoke, the words tangling on her tongue as she tried to explain why she was here. She imagined her secret spilling out, slipping like something live from her open mouth, the truth of her lunacy irrevocably revealed. And their pitying looks; the undercurrent of relief in their eyes as they silently exhaled, reassured that their own private madnesses were minor in comparison.

That won't happen, she told herself, and did not believe it. *I'm in control.* Her chest felt hollow, her ribs a fragile cage inside which unseen wings fluttered, quick and arrhythmic. A sudden lightness settled inside her head. *I'm in control*, she told herself again, approaching the door dry-mouthed.

A man was talking now. "I dream about my house catching fire," he said. "I always manage get out in time. Sometimes I'm able to save the kids, but never my wife. She's always stuck inside with the dog. I try to smash the windows but it's like they're made of diamond. I can see her at the top window, banging her hands against the glass. She's shouting, but I can't hear her, and I can't save her..." He broke off. His eyes were bright with tears, his voice suddenly thick. "I'm sorry," he managed, before pressing his sleeve to his mouth to stifle a sob.

That'll be you, a small voice inside of her insisted. *Don't go in there. You'll lose control. You'll panic. You'll probably pass out.*

She breathed deep, found her lungs utterly absent; an undignified splutter escaped her lips. She clapped a hasty palm over her mouth. A man in a pinstripe suit looked up from the circle, curious. There was something vaguely familiar about him, a sense that she'd seen him before. His eyes met hers through the gap in the door, black and inquisitive. She pulled sharply away, thumping against the wall; her fingers searched for something to hold on to, scrabbling fruitlessly against plaster. For a long moment she stood, palms flat against the wall, spine rigid, listening to the ebb and flow of conversation emanating from the open door. The ease of discussion astounded her, the revelation of fears and nightmares and memories, details which, to Alessa, seemed like pulling apart one's own ribcage and inviting the world to poke among the entrails.

"Excuse me?"

Alessa's heart lurched violently. She turned, wide-eyed, aware that her mouth was hanging open. The man in the pinstripe suit held up his hands, smiling apologetically. "Don't worry," he said. "I haven't come to tell you off for peeping. Actually, I should have left five minutes ago, but you get drawn in sometimes."

Embarrassment crept up her neck, colouring her cheeks. She forced her jaw shut. "I...I did want to come in," she said, turning her gaze to the buttons on his suit, the laces of his shoes, anywhere but his face. "I wasn't eavesdropping."

"It's okay. I believe you" He shoved his hands in his trouser pockets. He was very tall, perhaps six foot six and lanky with it. "It's a bit nerve-wracking the first few times. Takes a while to work up the courage. Trust me, you're not the only one ever to lurk out here for the entire session."

"How do you make yourself do it?" Alessa said suddenly.

He tilted his head, curious. "Do what?"

"That." She nodded towards the door, closed now since the man's exit. "In there. Everybody opening themselves up. Telling total strangers what keeps you awake at night. Don't you find it hard?"

"Honestly? No. But I'm used to performing on stage, and that's basically like standing naked in front of an auditorium full of people. Don't feel bad about it. It's not easy." He paused. "Anyway, I came out here because I sort of wanted to talk to you."

Cold dread settled beneath Alessa's skin. "Did you?"

"Yeah. It's just…I think I remember you," he said. "In the tunnel, after the bomb? You had glass…" he gestured vaguely in the general area of his thigh, like he was too squeamish to actually say it aloud. "Was that you?"

"Yes," Alessa said. She looked up at him, taking in his face for the first time. He was young – early twenties, maybe; olive skin, hair pulled back into a neat ponytail. High, sharp cheekbones, the kind of full, pretty lips women paid a fortune for. A model's face on a scarecrow's body. She cast her mind hesitantly back to the tunnel, to poor burnt Deborah and the woman with the silk scarf. It came to her, suddenly, a fuzzy memory, blurred at the edges like an old photograph. "You had a cello," she blurted, and was relieved when he smiled.

"I still have it," he said, a little shyly; he seemed hunch-shouldered and awkward, like he wasn't entirely sure what to do with all that height. "I have no idea how it didn't end up smashed to pieces. I guess it really does pay to get an expensive case. I'm Tom, by the way." He didn't extend his hand, and she was grateful for it. Her own were still trembling a little.

"Pleased to meet you," he said. "Briefly, anyway. I'm already running late for work and I really should get a move on instead of harassing you…"

"There was a man," Alessa said suddenly. "At the back of the train. He led me to safety. Probably others too." She forced herself to lift her chin, look Tom in the eye. He regarded her with placid interest. "Just before help came, he saw a light down in the

66

tunnel. It was coming from the direction of Elephant and Castle. He thought help had arrived and went to meet them, but…" The words were catching in her throat, threatening to tangle on her tongue. She swallowed hard. "I never saw him come back. I don't know what his name was. I don't know if he survived or not. It…it still bothers me."

There was a brief, thoughtful pause. She knotted her fingers tight; her knuckles bit sharply into one another.

"Look," Tom said, after a moment, glancing towards the door. "I really do need to go. But I think I remember that man. I remember watching him walk away." He fumbled in his shirt pocket and pulled out a business card. "You should email me. I can tell you everything I remember, for whatever it's worth."

She wanted to grab his sleeve and tell him to wait, to stay here and tell her everything, and she was sure he could see it in the desperate look on her face. But she held back, slipping the card into her pocket. "Okay," she said evenly. "Thank you. I'll be in touch."

A short while later Alessa found herself standing at the ticket barrier at Waterloo station, holding her Oyster card in one sweat-slick hand. She had intended it to be an act of empowerment, proof to herself that she could, but now she was actually here, breathing in the cold steel scent of the station, staring wide-eyed at the escalators leading down to the Tube platforms, she was beginning to question whether making a spur-of-the-moment decision powered solely by stubbornness had been a smart idea.

She took a deep breath and imagined black dust settling in her lungs. If she left it much longer it would soon be rush hour, and the crush of commuters would only make the experience worse. Her body seemed to run on automatic as she passed through the barriers and beyond, where the escalators rolled down into the depths.

It was quiet in the station. It had been quiet *that* day, too. She'd been half an hour later than she'd intended, although she couldn't remember *why*. She held onto that thought as she stepped into the lift, fixing her eyes on a faded poster for a musical that had finished the previous year. It seemed ludicrous that she could remember the exact position of every last stud of glass in the parka-woman's face, but not why she'd been late. Not the sole decision which had put her on that train, at that time.

Alessa closed her eyes.

People passed by her on the escalator. She could smell them, a fog of different perfumes and aftershaves and a faint hint of body odour, a cacophony of scents. She swallowed hard. She was stuck on this conveyor belt, sinking deep underground where the air was recycled through a hundred pairs of lungs before it ever reached your lips. *Jesus*, she thought as she stepped off the escalator, stomach lurching, *this was a terrible idea*.

Her feet moved, carrying her forward, and she let them go: around the corner, through the narrow corridors. She'd have been able to see the platform through the grilles if she were to look down, but she did not look down. She kept moving, walking without seeing until she was finally there.

The Bakerloo Line platform stretched out either side of her, once-white tiles rimmed with grey dirt. The posters here were the same ones she'd seen out of the train window that night, unchanged even in the month she'd stayed away. A little to her left was a bright, beautiful poster depicting some faraway beach, all sparkling turquoise sea and sapphire sky. She'd been staring longingly at that same poster when the train departed for Elephant and Castle that night, wondering how much two weeks in the Caribbean might cost.

The sign overhead indicated that the next train to Elephant and Castle was due in three minutes. A violent chill ran the length of her, settling in her gut. She would get on that train. She would do it to spite herself. To spite that little voice in her head that insisted she wasn't ready for this yet.

She looked around. Perched on the bench a few yards away was a woman with dyed black hair and a glimmering silver nose-ring, tapping a rolled-up copy of *Metro* impatiently against her knees. A little further down, a plump African woman garbed in jewel-bright fabric hummed cheerfully to herself. She thought about approaching one of them, but the idea seemed ridiculous.

What would she say? *Sorry to trouble you, but there's a better-than-average chance that I'll have a whopper of a panic attack the moment I set foot on this train, could you please hold my hand?* If she found herself on the verge of a meltdown she'd close her eyes, name the bones, and hope very hard that it would be enough.

The sign above the platform flashed: two minutes.

Alessa walked a little further along the platform. She couldn't bring herself to approach the yellow line. The platform stopped abruptly a few feet ahead, giving way to the black yawn of the tunnel. Unbidden, her mind conjured an image of the lost man – half a shadow in her mind, always in profile – shambling, dazed and bloody out of the tunnel like a zombie. She could imagine the looks on the faces of the passengers as he emerged from the stairwell, stinking of soot and blood and fear.

In the mouth of the tunnel, something moved.

Her head turned, an automatic motion, and she knew even as she moved that she didn't want to look. There seemed a sudden shiver of motion, a ripple in the darkness like a stone dropped into a perfectly still pond. She stood, transfixed, watching as the shadows danced in the deep, undulating with slow grace like kelp caught in some strange undertow. And she could *feel* them move, a low vibration reverberating deep in her spine, shuddering in the space between each vertebra.

She looked frantically around her. Nobody else seemed to notice anything amiss.

A pool of thick, tarry matter began to bleed out, long black fingers slithering along the rails, prying blindly at brickwork as they sought their way towards her. She took two faltering steps backwards, eyes fixed on the tunnel, tongue thick and dry in her mouth. In the depths, something seemed to pull, to twist, separating itself from the blackness around it as if the shadows were thick, viscous matter. It fell out onto the tracks, writhing maggotlike in the catchpit.

Occipital, she thought. *Parietal, frontal, temporal...*

A pair of pale eyes flickered open.

Alessa turned, gasping for air. The black-haired woman stared up at her. Beneath the thick kohl her eyes were hard as marbles. Alessa's heartbeat thundered in her throat, her nose, pulsing behind her eyes, and it was pure panic that made her run, a deep and intolerable terror which meant she did not stop when the woman spoke, quiet but audible even above the din of her own roaring blood:

"You see them too, don't you?"

FOUR

She thought she'd never be able to find her way back up, that the tunnels would curl in on themselves and lead in endless circles, burrowing ever deeper beneath the city. When she finally found herself in the concourse, staring at the sunlight through the grubby glass station roof, it seemed she had never felt such profound relief.

She headed outside, seeking fresh air and sky. The South Bank was a familiar place, and therefore a safe one. Even the crowds were reassuring. Dark things with pinhole eyes would surely not dare to lurk where they might be seen. She walked around the bridges, never under them where shadows convened and coagulated. On Waterloo Bridge she paused, filling her lungs with brackish air. She imagined she could see the soot of the Underground emerging from her mouth with every exhalation.

From above, the river seemed restless, churning debris around on the steely grey surface. When Alessa was younger, she had wondered if there might be something huge down there, cold and silent on the silt at the bottom, thrashing restlessly at the water. Some great, lonely monster.

You see them too, don't you?

The black-haired woman on the platform had opened the door to an awful possibility. Until now she'd been able to dismiss everything as some kind of hallucination, a 'monster in the closet' scenario borne out of panic. Not ideal, but it could be dealt with. It could be treated and resolved.

But if the black-haired woman had seen them too…

Her head suddenly seemed full of static. She managed to half-walk, half-stumble into the café adjacent, slipping into a seat at an empty table. She leaned back in her chair, breathing deep and slow. Her fingers trembled against the tabletop. The frantic hummingbird flutter of her heart had mostly subsided, though she could still hear the rush of her own blood, a faraway hiss like a seashell pressed to the ear.

I'm going to have a heart attack if I keep on like this, she thought, reaching for the coffee menu. She wondered what Moira would say about all of it. Surely this was a problem above and beyond the powers of meditation and aromatherapy.

"All right?"

Alessa looked up.

Slate-grey eyes stared back at her. The glint of a nose-ring. The dregs of adrenalin coursing through Alessa's system kicked up one last, faltering protest, but she was too tired to heed it.

"Don't run again," the black-haired woman warned, sliding casually into the seat opposite Alessa. Her voice was throaty, coarse, a dry wind scouring old bones. "I don't know what you think I'm all about but I swear I'm not gonna hurt you or nothing. I just want to talk."

Up close, she seemed comprised entirely of sharp angles; the bones of her face were severe, her nose like the edge of a hatchet. Her clothes hung from her thin frame in a way that suggested she'd deliberately bought them too big. Eyes like marbles set into the thin shell of her skull.

"How did you find me?"

The woman shrugged. "You don't move all that quickly. Plus you were sort of dazed. I've tracked trickier people."

"Right." Alessa wondered whether she made a habit out of tracking people. Something about the woman's face told her it wouldn't be a good idea to ask. "Why did you follow me?"

"I wanted to talk," the woman replied. Her skin seemed translucent, the web of her veins visible at her temples. "About what happened in the station. You going off like a rocket and all that."

"I was hurt in the Elephant and Castle bombing," Alessa said. She found herself talking quietly, which was ridiculous; the people around her probably didn't give a shit about her personal circumstances. "It was the first time I'd been on the Tube since the explosion. I panicked."

"Didn't you just," the woman said. She leaned across the table. She smelled of rollup cigarettes, a deep, pungent odour. "Listen," she said. "I know what really happened. You panicked, but not because you got triggered or whatever. It was the thing in the tunnel. The *shade*." She almost spat out the last word. "You're scared," the woman said, though Alessa thought she'd been doing an admirable job of remaining stone-faced. "'Course you are, it's not every day you see spooks hanging about in the shadows. But I've been seeing them for a while now. Ever since the bomb."

You're mad, Alessa thought. And she did look it; her eyes had taken on a manic sheen, her cheeks flushed a feverish pink. And if she was mad, that meant Alessa was almost certainly mad too. At least she wasn't alone. The thought was oddly comforting.

The woman leant in closer. The tip of her nose almost brushed Alessa's chin; she moved backwards with a jolt. "You've probably told yourself they're a figment of your imagination. You've tried to forget about them. I did too, at first. But I *know* you want to know what they are." She spoke in the hushed tones of one imparting some great and profound secret. "You're asking yourself, can they hurt me?"

"Can they?" Alessa asked.

The woman drew back, adopting the same slack-shouldered posture she'd had when she first sat down. She was still flushed, but there was something predatory about her expression now, a certain satisfaction; she'd baited the hook and known Alessa would bite. "We shouldn't talk about it here," she said. "Bit public, innit? Take my phone number. Ring me later on, when you've had time to calm down." She put out her hand and Alessa found herself handing over her mobile, watching as the woman jabbed at the screen.

Alessa looked over at the bar, wondering if it was too early for gin. She wasn't sure about this woman. She was an unknown quantity, and Alessa had always preferred the safe and familiar. But she claimed to hold information that Alessa badly wanted to know, and her burning curiosity was fast winning out over her uncertainty.

"Here," she said, handing the phone back over. Alessa glanced at it. The woman's fingers had left faint smudges on the screen. There was a mobile number and above it, in capital letters, the name 'CASEY'.

The woman stood abruptly. "Ring whenever," she said. "I don't really sleep, so you won't be disturbing me."

"Right," Alessa said, staring at the screen. "I'm Alessa, by the way."

Casey tipped her a nod. "A pleasure," she said. "Ring me." She jabbed a brief finger in the direction of Alessa's phone and then she was gone, slipping out of the door and into the crowd with such ease that Alessa almost wondered if she'd been there at all.

*

It was still light outside when Alessa got home. She grabbed her laptop from under the coffee table and booted it up. Her wallpaper was a picture Shannon had taken a few years ago during one of her frequent 'spiritual' sojourns to Ibiza; a surprisingly adept photograph of Es Vedra at sunset, sky and sea merged into a single bright pool of burning amber. It occurred to her just how badly she needed a holiday.

There was a raft of unread emails in her inbox, mostly money off vouchers for restaurants she never ate at. She clicked 'Compose Mail' and rummaged among the lint and receipts in her pocket for the card Tom had given her earlier.

Her hands hovered over the keyboard. What was she supposed to say? She hated emails almost as much as she hated phoning people; there was something sterile and unpleasant about communicating without the benefit of body language. Keep it simple, she told herself.

To: kallemdjiantom@gmail.com
CC:
Subject:

Hello Tom, this is Alessa Spiteri. I met you at the Healing Hearts support group earlier today and you suggested I should email you. We talked about the man we both saw that night on the Underground.

I hope I'm not disturbing you. Thank you for taking the time to speak with me about this.

Best,
Alessa.

She clicked 'Send' and set the laptop back on the coffee table.

Alessa glanced around the bombsite of rubbish that constituted the living room and kitchen. She had never intended to live this way. It had crept up on her quietly, the way old age and infirmity inevitably would. For the first couple of weeks after the bomb she'd been too sore and too shell-shocked to do much more than lurk around the house like a sad, listless ghost. And the rubbish had slowly taken over. The black bags out on the balcony had resembled a Tracy Emin installation. Towels and clothes lay in sad little piles on the floor, as if their occupants had been suddenly spirited away. By the time she felt able to get back to the business of actually *living*, the flat was in such a pitiful state that the thought of tackling it all made her want to lie down in a dark room. The task didn't seem so horribly insurmountable any more. She supposed that might be a sign of progress.

Alessa rooted through the kitchen in search of something edible, realising with dismay that it had been a long time since she'd been to the supermarket. She surfaced with a slightly stale packet of cream crackers, a mostly empty tub of cheese spread and an unopened jar of green olives which, judging by the film of dust coating the glass, had been languishing in the cupboard for quite some time.

She was assembling her meal when her mobile rang, buzzing loud on the coffee table. It was probably Shannon, calling to see how she'd got on at the support group. Alessa grabbed the phone, swiped the screen with her thumb. "Yep?" she said, hurriedly swallowing a mouthful of cheese-laden cracker.

"Are you talking with your mouth full? That's nasty."

That voice, dry as old earth. "Casey? How'd you get my number?"

"I rang myself from your phone. Earlier, in the café. Surprised you never noticed." Alessa could almost hear the shrug in her voice. She was resolutely laconic, as if words were currency she didn't want to spend. "D'you wanna hear about the Shades or not?"

"I didn't think you meant I should call as soon as I got home." Alessa said. "I haven't even had dinner yet."

"You're eating right now."

"I'm eating cream crackers and Dairylea," she said. "Er. With olives on. I'm not convinced that counts as 'dinner'."

She heard Casey snort. "Classy," she said. "Look, I'm loath to invite myself into the houses of strangers, but I've got a booklet of Domino's vouchers, and I'm just saying, but I think if you're gonna go for the bread-cheese-olives combo you might as well do it properly."

Alessa glanced at her squalid surroundings. Casey was offering two things, both of which she badly needed: company, and answers. And while she was not usually in the habit of inviting people into her flat after a five-minute conversation, there was also the fact that it would soon be dark, and she would be alone again, hiding from whatever lurked in the car park.

"Give me an hour," Alessa said.

*

Within forty minutes Alessa had cleared several weeks' worth of rubbish, scrubbed most of the surfaces and loaded the washing machine. She'd even found the energy to take three lots of black bags down to the communal bins. The sky had turned a deep blue, darkening on the eastern horizon. Once her business was done, she retreated back into the safety of her well-lit flat, peering over her shoulder as she went; no trace of strange shadows, no monsters lurking in unlit corners.

It felt faintly euphoric, this sudden energy, and for a short while she forgot about the bomb, and the light in the tunnel, and everything that had followed. The residual ache of her thigh was the only thing tethering her to that memory. It was like emerging from a thick fog and finding herself somewhere new and exciting, and she couldn't quite believe that Casey was the catalyst. She was a stranger, and somewhat odd to boot, but she was currently the only person in the world Alessa felt she could be honest with.

Alessa pulled all the curtains shut at seven PM. She did not glance down into the car park, or beyond it to where the imposing black outline of the Rockingham Estate stood. She would be braver when Casey was here, she told herself.

She almost jumped out of her skin when the buzzer echoed loudly throughout the flat.

"Pizza delivery," came Casey's dour voice through the intercom.

When she arrived at the door, she was dressed in an unseasonably thick duffel coat and too-big beanie hat. Two large pizza boxes rested on the shelf of her forearms, the smell of hot grease and pepperoni drifting upwards. "You're not a veggie, are you?" Casey asked, moving past Alessa into the hall. "'Cause there's about six types of dead animal in here and I'm not taking it back."

Alessa was mildly taken aback by her brazenness, but amused too. She followed her into the living room, watching as Casey glanced briefly around the flat. "No, I'm not a vegetarian."

"Good. Pizza without ground beef is an abomination. You want these on the coffee table, or are you a knife-and-fork sort of person?"

"God, no."

Casey smiled, revealing tiny pebble-teeth. "I think we're going to be friends."

They made small talk over pizza and blackcurrant squash. Whether by accident or design Casey was guarded, revealing little about herself; she lived locally, was 'productively unemployed', had accumulated Domino's vouchers through 'more custom than is healthy'. She'd been heading to the trauma group the previous day but had bottled out at the last minute, and had ended up sitting in the station for half an hour instead, watching the creatures lurking in the tunnel. That was the most Alessa had been able to prise out of Casey, and she did not begrudge her. They barely knew one another.

"Okay, so listen," Casey said, wiping her hands on her jeans. "What you saw in the station. You ever seen that before?"

Alessa picked olives off her slice and popped them into her mouth. "The shadow-things? Yes," she said. It occurred to her that this was an insane conversation, that there was a good chance Casey was some kind of paint-sniffing lunatic. "I've never seen them appear like that. The other times they just seemed to be *there*."

"Not every day you get to witness the birth of a brand new baby Shade," Casey said. "It's an, uh, what do they call it? An *auspicious* occasion. I've only ever seen it a handful of times myself. Little shit's probably lurking in the tunnels now. Why are your curtains drawn?"

"I thought they'd stay away if they couldn't see me," she said, a little sheepish. Casey just nodded, brow furrowed and serious. "Don't. They don't like light. Keep your curtains open. Put your lights on when it gets dark. They'll keep their distance."

"What *are* they?"

"That's the million dollar question, innit?" She paused, plucking at a pizza crust. "Here's the thing. I'm not an expert or nothing, but I've been watching them. For the first week or so I only ever saw them around near where the bomb went off. A little while after that, I saw them down in the tunnels after a seriously messy suicide at St Pauls. My best guess is that they're somehow attracted to areas of emotional trauma. I think that's why we see them."

"Because of the bomb?"

Casey nodded. "Because of the bomb. Think about how much raw emotion gets kicked up after something like that. I mean, you've got grief and pain and fear and all kinds of bad juju, and they're *all* about that, you know, the way moths are with lights.

But here's where it gets interesting. See, from what I've seen, Shades prefer to stay hidden, but when they get a whiff of personal trauma they get brave. Or stupid, maybe. They seem to go after it. You get me?"

"Sort of."

"What I *mean* is, I don't know if you were having a shitty time beforehand or if the bomb just really took it out of you, but the Shades've taken an interest in whatever emotional baggage you're carrying. That's why you're seeing them everywhere. You're basically leaving a breadcrumb trail, and they're following it."

Alessa sank deep into the sagging sofa cushions, staring at the gap in the curtains. The story Casey was spinning was convincing enough to Alessa, whose 'emotional baggage', at this point, could have comfortably filled the back of a van. But it was also insane.

"Why tube stations, though?" She watched Casey lob a bunched-up tissue neatly into an open pizza box. "Bad things happen all over London, all the time. Do they only go above ground to follow someone?"

"Far as I know," Casey said. She was curled in the corner of the sofa, feet tucked beneath her. She'd taken no time at all in making herself at home. "This is all guesswork, remember, and, full disclosure, a lot of it happened at three in the morning. Insomnia's a bitch." She fumbled in her coat pocket – still draped across her shoulders, although she'd slipped her arms free, the sleeves hanging loose and empty – and pulled out a green pouch of Golden Virginia tobacco. "As for the Underground...there's a guy I know, he harps on about this thing called the Stone Tape theory. They reckon that stone retains psychic trauma better than any other medium. Let's say for a minute that he's not a total bloody lunatic. When you consider the *genesis* of the Underground, all the plague pits dug up when the tunnels went in, all the people killed during construction, and then all the shit that happened after, like the stampede at Bethnal Green during the war. All that would be absorbed and stored. It'd become part of the fabric of the Underground. You ever heard any of the ghost stories they tell about the Tube?"

"Footsteps on the platform when there's nobody around, that sort of thing?"

Casey nodded, extracting a roll-up from the pouch. It dangled unlit between her fingers. "Okay, so the theory goes that what we think are the souls of the dead are actually just echoes. Recordings, you get me? If someone dies a really violent or traumatic death, all that bad juju is absorbed by their surroundings and what you get is almost like a film. Those last moments of their lives, playing out on a loop for eternity. That'd be why ghosts seem to repeat the same course of action over and over."

Golden strands of loose tobacco speckled the newly-hoovered sofa. Alessa swallowed her dismay. "Do you actually believe that?" she asked.

"Dunno," Casey said. "It's just a theory. I could be well off the mark. The only solid facts I know is that the Shades are actually real, that I started seeing them after the bomb, and that they've been following me about ever since. Same as you, I guess. Everything else is conjecture."

"Why do you keep calling them 'Shades'? Is that what they're really called?"

Casey snorted. "I don't bloody know. It's not like you can just Google them. When you're dealing with stuff that doesn't officially exist, you sort of have to bring your own vocabulary to the party. The Stone Tape Theory guy came up with it. It's some kind of nerdy Greek literature reference. He took offence to me calling them 'lamprey bastards'. You know, 'cos of the teeth?"

Alessa thought of the shadow-thing she'd seen in the car park. The black hole of its mouth, crammed with teeth like shards of shattered glass. She wondered how easily they might pierce flesh. Whether they could crunch through bone. "Yeah," she said. Her skin prickled with sudden gooseflesh. "They look nasty."

"*Nasty*," Casey repeated, with some satisfaction. She produced a lighter from her coat pocket. "You mind?" she asked, waving her roll-up. When Alessa shook her head, she lit up, pulling the empty pizza box towards her to use as an ashtray. "Fucking horrifying is more like it," she said, through a mouthful of cigarette. "First time I saw them I was insensible for a week. Second time was better. I've got a high tolerance for weird shit." She smoked silently for a moment, puffing out misshapen smoke rings. They dissipated slowly as they rose to the ceiling. "But it's normal to be freaked out by all this, you know? It feels your mind has suddenly checked out, especially the first time you see one."

"I was on the bus." Alessa said. Her stomach suddenly felt uncomfortably full, the room too small. She forced herself to breathe, slow and steady. "In the window. I thought it was a shadow but it had *eyes*, and they were looking right at me. And I panicked. I shut my eyes and told myself it was all in my head, and when I opened them again it was gone. And then...I felt ridiculous."

"It's all right to panic," Casey said, so suddenly that Alessa was startled despite the softness of her voice. "I think that actually proves you're still sane."

"I assumed it was stress," Alessa said. Her fingers were an awkward bundle of bones in her lap; she focused on the interplay of muscle and tendon, anything to stop her from bursting into tears. "I just couldn't reconcile what I'd seen in any other way. It couldn't possibly be real, so it must have been PTSD, right? But the second time I saw one, it didn't disappear. I didn't want to believe what I was seeing, but it was right there, just…just sort of standing. And it wasn't frightened of me. That was the worst part. It looked right up at me and I knew I was the only one of us that was afraid."

She felt the gentle pressure of Casey's hand on her arm; a brief, reassuring squeeze.

"But you're not on your own anymore," Casey said. Her eyes were dark in the lamplight. There was a awful loneliness behind them, a sort of earnest desperation in the way she held Alessa's arm. It seemed to Alessa that Casey probably didn't have anybody, and Alessa was her sole, tenuous link to the rest of the world. "You and me, we're gonna sort this out. We'll be okay. And I don't know how, but I promise you this: I'm gonna work out how to get rid of the bastards forever."

*

Casey left at eleven. Alessa wasn't sure she liked the idea of someone so small and fragile-looking walking home by herself that late at night, but Casey waved away her concerns, cigarette smoke pluming out from her grin-split mouth. "Anyone jumps me, I'll knock their teeth so far down their throat they'll be shitting enamel for a week," Casey said, and Alessa believed her. She'd always thought she was tough and self-reliant, that she could cope with all number of hardships without anyone's help, but watching Casey – the way she held herself, straight-shouldered, no small amount of swagger despite her diminutive frame – she realised she'd been dead wrong.

When Casey was gone, Alessa scooped up her mobile. The screen indicated a new message; she swiped with her thumb to open it. It was from Shannon.

Jst saw 3 kids on Boris bikes doin wheelies up Tooley Street. Knobheads. How r u? Support grp ok?

She'd sent the message at 8.14pm, which was shortly after Casey had arrived. Alessa unbuttoned her trousers with one hand and kicked them off as she walked into the bedroom, texting Shannon back with her free hand. Her thumb worked clumsily over the keyboard:

Wasn't my thing. Not going back. Met a couple of interesting people though, might know something about the man in the tunnel, so not a complete waste of time.

Shannon would be disappointed. She always was when one of her suggestions fell flat, like the time she'd suggested they both try a 'juice detox' and by the end of the first day Alessa had been so ravenously hungry she would have happily eaten the sofa.

Alessa went into the windowless bathroom and turned on the light. The low buzz of the extractor fan kicked in like a faraway plane taking off. She shucked off the rest of her clothes, catching sight of the too-prominent swell of her stomach in the mirror as she leaned over to turn on the shower, the slight sag of her heavy breasts. Once upon a time, not so long ago, she'd hated that reflection, disgusted with the softness of her body. An ex-boyfriend's offhanded comment had become a full-blown complex; by the time that boyfriend had packed his bags she'd grown too afraid of her own unclothed body to find another. In the wake of the bomb - bruised and trembling, the great, ugly scar adjacent to her thigh bone still pink and prominent – she'd realised just how ridiculous her perception had been.

Her phone buzzed. She scooped it up from the corner of the sink, peering through the fast-gathering steam at the message:

Cant u give it 1 more try? I bet u never even gave it a chance! U have 2 be willin 2 let ppl help u.

Yeah, yeah, thought Alessa, rolling her eyes. Well, she was letting people help her, though perhaps it wasn't quite what Shannon was alluding to. But sitting around sharing sob stories wasn't the kind of help she needed. What she needed was answers.

What she needed was to know she wasn't going insane.

FIVE

She woke the next morning to a text from Shannon and an email from Tom. Bleary-eyed, she tackled the text first:

Gene Kelly marathon on Sky 2nite. Come rnd? Ill gt snax in x x

She sat up. It had been a while since she'd last slept that deeply, undisturbed by the strange dreams that had been plaguing her since the bomb. Her limbs felt heavy, a little sore from having been stuck in the same position she'd fallen asleep in. It took her a moment to decipher the tiny text of Tom's email:

Hey Alessa,

Glad you emailed. I really don't know how much help I can be but I'll do whatever I can. Meet for coffee or something? There's a place called Coffee Minute opposite the shopping centre that's pretty easy for me to get to – nothing fancy but it'll give us somewhere relatively private to talk. I'm free this evening if that's any good to you?

Tom

As Alessa fired back an email confirming the meeting, she realised she felt no spark of excitement at the prospect of tying up this loose end. All this time she had fixated on the man in the tunnel; he had been the centrepiece to all of her nightmares, the one constant in every flashback. And how strange that now, standing on the precipice of a fresh lead, she should find her interest suddenly waning.

It wasn't that she didn't care anymore. She knew that with certainty. The mystery of his disappearance still gnawed at her with that same lunatic intensity, her illogical need for an irrelevant answer no more likely to soothe her trauma than a plaster would heal a bullet-hole. But there was a fresh layer of noise inside her head now, a fear she could substantiate even less: the shadow-things in the periphery of her vision, edging ever closer, and the spectre of her own insanity brought sharply into focus by these bizarre apparitions.

And of course, there was Casey, and her mad theories, as compelling as they were utterly divorced from reality. Casey, who listened to her and believed her, and who had suddenly become the closest thing she had to a friend.

Alessa peeled herself out of bed, letting the month-old bedsheets lay in a heap. The queasy smell of stale pizza crust and old grease hit her as she entered the living room, the boxes lying empty on the coffee table. When she sat on the sofa, the faint odour of Golden Virginia tobacco drifted up from the fabric.

She opened the windows a crack and replied to Shannon: *Much as I'd love to indulge your love of dead actors, I'm out this evening x*

The reply was almost instantaneous:

Wooo is this a date or sth? gimme details

She rolled her eyes. Shannon was insistent that Alessa couldn't possibly be happy single and ought to 'put herself out there' – an appallingly meat-market turn of phrase. It wasn't that Alessa never felt lonely, but watching Shannon negotiate a painful and complicated divorce the previous year had left her less than enthusiastic about entering into that kind of commitment. Her sister was not best placed to be dishing out relationship advice.

No date. Someone I met at the support group. We're going out for coffee and trauma talk.

Shannon replied: *@ least tell me hes fit*

She knew enough about her sister's taste in men to determine that Tom was exactly her type. Alessa responded: *not my type. Tall pretty boy w/ bambi eyes. You'd like him though.*

There was a minute's pause before the reply:

Can I come 2?

*

By the time Alessa left the flat it was already growing dark again; her existence had become accidentally crepuscular, flitting from darkness to darkness as if quietly allergic to the sun. The lights in the stairwell were defective, flickering like flashbulbs and casting long shadows on the opposite wall.

The car park smelled of day-old fried chicken, fox piss, and petrol leaking from a derelict Ford Focus which, judging by the rusted wheel-arches and total absence of headlights, had not functioned for quite some time. Alessa stuck close to the streetlamps, aware of the way her shadow shifted and warped; her limbs appeared elongated and strangely languid, like an alien. Like a Shade, she thought, rolling the word around in her mind.

Coffee Minute was a little way north of the shopping centre, which meant navigating the dimly-lit labyrinth of underpasses beneath the roundabout. Alessa had always felt relatively safe down there in the daytime, but the lights would frequently splutter and die without warning. At the intersection between two tunnels, a homeless man wearing a threadbare blue beanie lay wrapped in a sleeping bag; a tuft of squirrel-grey beard peeked out. A carpet of cardboard was spread out beneath him, warped at the edges with damp. She fished in her pockets for spare change and came up empty.

Alessa deliberately avoided the station, choosing to walk on the opposite side of the road. A fractured spine of red plastic fencing formed an untidy ring around an excavation which, to Alessa's memory, had been there for well over a year, uninterrupted and unworked on. So much of the area was heavily under development now. Her mother had complained recently that she barely recognised Elephant and Castle anymore, what with all the new-build flats springing up like weeds, and the demolition of the old housing estates.

Gentrification was a slow but persistent process; the Elephant seemed to resisting quite admirably, but it was a losing battle. The expensive new-builds came with coffee shops built in, and a rash of boutiques and delis seemed to be sprouting like fungus all over the place. But for every artisan sandwich bar that appeared, three more chicken shops followed, annexing the newcomer with landfill quantities of empty cardboard containers and meat-stripped bones in the gutter. Regeneration would not happen here without a fight.

She hadn't even known there was a coffee shop here, but there it was, all black sign and gold lettering, peering out from the shadow of a towering residential block. Two shops down, a grubby red-and-white sign for

Perfect Fried Chicken glowed reassuringly in the gloom.

A blast of warm air enveloped her as she stepped inside. The coffee shop was not quite full but a low wall of chatter presided, a pleasant hum of indistinct noise. She scanned the shop for Tom's ponytail. She sighted him somewhere near the back and lifted her hand in tentative greeting, sidling around marshmallowy leather sofas. He smiled when she slid into the chair opposite. It was the kind of disarming, lopsided smile that, under different circumstances, she might have found charming.

"I'm really glad you could make it," he said. There was a half-finished cappuccino on the table before him, and next to it a tall, steaming latte in a glass mug. She assumed he'd ordered it for her. Lattes were generally a safe bet if you didn't know someone's coffee preference. "I'm sorry for running off like that yesterday. My boss is really understanding but the work doesn't do itself."

"What do you do?"

"I'm an accountant."

Alessa whistled through her teeth. "I'm sorry."

That disarming smile again. If Shannon were here she'd have melted a thousand times over by now. He had big, calm eyes, so dark they seemed to lack colour entirely. "You'd miss us if we disappeared," he said. "All that paperwork you'd have to do. What about you? What exciting career choice did you make?"

"I was a teaching assistant," she said. "At a primary school."

"Sounds wild," Tom said.

"I was let go from my last job," she admitted. She raised her fingertips to the glass, letting the heat of it warm her skin. "I'm reapplying to the agency but it might be hard finding work, what with all the..." she almost said *hallucinations* but caught herself in time. "...well, you know," she finished, waving a dismissive hand.

"You can talk about it," he said, lowering his voice. "About the things you see. I know all about it."

A sudden chill crept beneath her skin. "I'm not sure what you mean."

"Best not be drinking my latte," came Casey's voice from over her shoulder. "I've cut bitches for less." She turned, saw Casey approaching from the other side of the shop. She was bundled up despite the warmth of the shop, a white woolen scarf wrapped loose around her throat. She slipped into the seat beside Tom, offering Alessa a brief flash of a smile. "Sorry about that," she said. "Coffee's a diuretic, innit? I'd have wet myself if I'd waited for you to get here."

"What are you..." her eyes flickered between Tom and Casey, between her grey, flinty eyes and Tom's darker, prettier features. Neither seemed troubled by the other's presence. It was as if they'd arranged the whole thing between them.

"We met at the trauma group," Casey said. "Tom was the only one who didn't think I was completely mental. Mostly because he's seen the Shades too."

Alessa forced herself to remain neutral. "Have you?"

"I'm the reason she calls them Shades in the first place," Tom said, stirring brown sugar into his cappuccino. Whorls of dark coffee cut through the thick foam. "Homer's

Odyssey. Bit nerdy, but it's better than 'lamprey bastards'."

"Because of the teeth," Casey said, solemn.

"Casey did an artist's impression for me once" Tom said, hushed, as if it were confidential information. "She's right. It's creepy as hell."

"You've never seen the teeth?" Alessa asked.

Casey looked at him expectantly, tilting her head. "I only saw them once," Tom said, after a moment. "I thought I was concussed, if I'm honest. It was shortly after that man went down the tunnel to get help. You'd already been evacuated by then – you were hurt worse than some of us. When I was waiting for them to come and get me, I looked down into the tunnel and they were there. Three of them. They were a long way down. I remember just staring at them – I could barely make them out, except for the eyes. Like thin men crouching in the dark. They were just staring, you know, not even doing anything. And I started to freak out…not even because of what I was seeing, but because it felt like my head was about to explode. I could smell blood and soot and

burnt hair, and I could hear *everything.*
Every footstep." He fiddled compulsively
with a packet of sugar, fingers worrying at
the edges. "Every scream."

"Do you think they followed him down
there?"

Had they been attracted so quickly to the
scene of the accident? The thought of those
spindly creatures - their long, malformed
limbs, stalking the man quietly through the
black of the tunnel - sent a prickle of
gooseflesh up Alessa's arms.

"Who knows?" Casey licked a thin layer of
milk foam from her lips, tongue small and
kittenlike. "Did you ever check to see if he
was listed as being unaccounted for?"

"I recall him saying he'd only recently
arrived in the country," Tom said. "Probably
nobody ever reported him missing. I didn't
see anything about it in the news
afterwards."

"Could be that he saw them following him.
It'd shit anybody up. Maybe he got out fine,
he's just too scared to leave the house."

"I doubt it," Alessa said. She was aware of
the proximity of the other tables, how easily

their conversation might carry. How crazy they'd sound if it did.

"Why?" Casey said, quirking a lazy eyebrow. "Almost happened to you, didn't it?"

She couldn't answer that.

"Anyway," Casey said, straightening up in her seat. "You're probably thinking 'why the bloody hell is this nutter even here?' And I'll tell you. Better still, I'll *show* you." She patted at the pockets of her jacket, pulling out a yellow plastic lighter. When she stood up, she was only a little taller than Tom. She patted him on the shoulder. "I need a smoke first, though. Shall we, Mr Kallemdjian?"

"Sure." Tom scooted out from his chair, unfolding to his full height, awkwardly hunched and heronlike. Beside him, Casey was almost laughably tiny. And yet Casey, utterly insubstantial even in her oversized khaki jacket and loose jeans, was a study in confidence against the odds; tiny doll-limbs, face sharp as a knife-edge.

"Where are we going?" Alessa asked, swallowing down her other objections: *what are you doing here, did you plan this, can I trust you?*

"To see what we can see," Casey said. "Don't worry, this isn't some kind of weird double con. We're not going to jump you and goat-tie you up in an alley somewhere. Trust me, okay? You're going to want to see this."

They spilled out of Coffee Minute in a glut of bodies. Despite the onward march of spring, the air was still sharp and chilly; Alessa tucked her hands into the armpits of her parka, breathing white in the dark as Casey led them up Walworth Road, past the Vietnamese supermarket, shutters adorned with graffiti; tags layered upon tags until they were barely distinguishable from one another. Casey smoked in silence, puffing grey plumes out between thin lips, leading the procession with Tom close behind her. They exchanged idle chatter with the easy informality of old friends, though they couldn't have known one another long. Alessa noted the way Tom's eyes fixed intently on Casey's face, drinking in the hard symmetry of her features. *Jesus*, she thought, *but what does he see in her?*

She was taken aback by her own spite and quickly ducked her head, hiding the hot flush of shame that crept up her neck. It was none of her damn business anyway; they were both adults. She lagged behind, wanting to trust them but maintaining a comfortable distance. Just in case, she told herself.

The roar of rush-hour traffic from the main road had subsided to a low, steady hum, growing fainter as they walked down Rodney Place and round, out onto Heygate Street, where the stream of cars was more intermittent, and the darkness more profound. The air smelled wet and lush, an abundance of damp leaves overhead from the towering plane trees lining the road – the sole remnants of the 'Urban Forest' which, to Alessa, had always seemed little more than just a clot of overlarge trees in dire need of a trim.

"Here," Casey said, and indicated a loose patch of wire tucked away behind the jut of a brick wall. She held it aside while Tom and Alessa wriggled through. Yellow signs proclaimed the presence of guard dogs, but the building site looked entirely deserted to

Alessa's eyes; all activity was concentrated on the farthest end, near the railway bridge, where the bare bones of a new apartment block stood, stark and skeletal in the bright floodlights.

They were swallowed by the darkness, skirting huge piles of rubble hidden beneath great black tarpaulins; Alessa thought they resembled the bodies of dead giants. Loose chunks of brick rolled beneath her feet. Her head rolled with them, pulsing as if with some terrible pressure. This was madness. Why was she following two near-strangers onto a building site this late in the evening? Trespassing in this quiet, isolated place, where they might do anything to her, and nobody would know?

Alessa shut her eyes, drew in a deep breath; the air tasted of damp, mildewed stone. The faint scent of fried electrics filtered up, the crisp pork-crackling smell of burnt human flesh. Somewhere in the distance, someone was screaming. *This isn't real*, she told herself, swallowing down a thick, sour wave of nausea. *Nobody's screaming. Nobody's burning. Open your eyes.*

She did. There was only Casey, looking at her quizzically. "You all right?" she asked.

"Why are we here?" Alessa's voice seemed to carry a long way in the quiet. Remnants of a central green peeked up through the shattered concrete, long fronds of grass whispering against her jeans.

"I've seen them here," Casey said. "Two nights running, lurking around the rubble."

Alessa frowned. "If they gravitate towards the Underground like you said before, what's drawing them to the Heygate?"

"All kinds of history in these bricks," Casey said. "Decades' worth. They were supposed to knock this estate down ages ago, you know. And it's been held back over and over. They're almost there but they're holding back on these last couple of structures for some weird reason. The latest excuse is asbestos. But you can feel it, can't you? Soon as the sun goes down, this place clears out. You think that's coincidental?"

"Casey," Tom said, a little wearily. "They haven't delayed the demolition because of the bloody Shades."

"Not as far as they know, no." Casey seemed unflustered, her conviction unbent.

"But that doesn't mean it isn't true. Maybe they justify it in their heads some other way. Just like you blamed what happened to you in the tunnel on a concussion." She looked faintly triumphant, as if her logic could not possibly be contested. And why not? Maybe there was a deliberate pall cast across this place. A low-key dread emanating like radio waves from one singular point.

It was only Tom's mildly puzzled expression that made Alessa realise she'd said the last part out loud.

Casey nodded, head bobbing frantically. "You can feel something's wrong, but you don't know why. There are a lot of places like that in this city, and nobody ever connects it to anything supernatural. It's just...a certain vibe, that this is not a good place. And it's them, you know. They get inside your head. Amplify all of your worst thoughts. Make you feel like you're going insane."

Alessa thought of Loman Street. The keening of the alarm and the shadows pooled in the gaps between the streetlamps, cold as ocean trenches. The sensation of something thin and unnatural, just out of sight, and the paranoia crawling beneath her skin. *They get inside your head.*

"Why do you think only we can see them?" she asked.

"I don't think anyone's supposed to," Tom said. He kicked a chunk of concrete with the toe of his shoe. It rolled a short distance, coming to an abrupt halt a yard or so away. "My guess is it's related to Casey's trauma theory. Whatever it is they get out of negative emotional energy – some kind of euphoric state, maybe - it's got to be worth breaking cover for. Could even be addictive."

"You're assuming it's a conscious choice," Casey said. She turned, walking momentarily backwards. "Maybe there's some kind of inbuilt imperative that dictates the way they behave. They seek out trauma because they can't *not* do it. Y'know, maybe they feed off it. Maybe it sustains them."

Somewhere in the distance, the plaintive whine of an ambulance siren sparked into being.

"Anyway, listen. Nobody goes off on their own," Casey said. "All right? We're dealing with the unknown, so we do this properly."

She turned to Alessa, nodding curtly. "You stick with me, follow my lead. I'm here to keep you safe."

Something rustled in the trees behind them. Alessa turned sharply, staring out into the distance. Just the wind, she told herself, although the cliché offered scant comfort. The street lights out on the main road bathed the treetops in rich, ruddy gold. Elongated shadows mingled with the strange lunar landscape, playing off the ruined bricks.

The logical part of Alessa's mind screamed at her to turn around. That even if there were shadow-things here, hiding among the rubble, no good would come of encountering them. And yet the other part of her – the part which seemed to draw from Casey's courage and defiance and utter refusal to let the Shades win – almost *wanted* to see them. *Come out*, she thought, though her fingers twitched ceaselessly with anxiety. *Let's meet on my terms. Let's see what you're about.*

They were nearing the tall black shape to the rear of the site, one of the few structures still standing. The windows had been boarded up a long time ago, the facade

116

bedecked with such an abundance and variety of graffiti that it all seemed to blend into one huge vortex of colour and shape; tags blazing in bright paint, a futile bid to be the last name standing when the building finally fell to the bulldozers. Two-thirds of the block had already been demolished. Damp wallpaper was exposed to the elements, a patchwork of colour and pattern incongruous against the grey concrete. Remnants of a life. In the distance, aborted walkways sprung up out of the night; staircases to nowhere, and beneath them, garage doors jimmied open and gaping like mouths.

Alessa still remembered the walkways running the length of the estate like a great arterial loop; she remembered her mother telling her and Shannon that they must never use the Heygate as a shortcut, that they might get mugged or worse up on those high, isolated walkways. She and Shannon would deliberately walk through the Heygate just to defy her; she remembered the terrible thrill of footsteps on the stairs behind them, the glimpse of a face staring up at them from below as they scurried through.

The front door of the ground floor flat was tucked away inside an alcove. Like all the other flats the front door had been covered with a thick steel safety door designed to keep squatters out, but some enterprising soul had prised it free. It now sat propped at a close angle, covering the gaping hole where the original door had once been.

"I've got a torch," Casey said, voice low. She held it aloft. "They're close. Can't you smell them?"

Alessa inhaled. It was a sour, fermented smell, old milk laced with vinegar, and her stomach lurched uneasily as Casey eased though the gap left by the safety door, followed by Tom. Was this what the Shades smelled like, or was it just the abandoned flat decomposing slowly around her? Tom waited for her to squeeze through the doorway, face wan in the pale light emanating from his phone. He gave her an encouraging smile, and there was an uncomfortable cheeriness to it, his mouth creased a little too wide. He almost looked excited to be here.

Directly to the left was the remnants of a kitchen, though all the fittings had been taken; even the kitchen sink was gone, leaving a hole in the worktop like a missing tooth. Waterlogged lino peeled back off the concrete floor, grey at the edges with mould. Ahead, the stairs led up to a lightless landing. Casey's torch beam disappeared into deep blue oblivion. Loose plaster lay in great chunks on each step, hacked out of the wall by what could only have been human hands.

"This way," Casey said, indicating that they should follow. They passed into the living-room, wide and empty save for a waterlogged cardboard box set against the far wall. Dust motes danced lazily before their torch beams. An empty windowframe stood where sliding doors ought to have been, leading out onto a cracked patio teeming with overgrown plant pots. A trellis was arranged against the wall, choked with what might have been a particularly virulent strain of ivy. Beyond the gaps in the fence lay a cratered vista of ruined concrete, fissures seemingly depthless in shadow, the dull glow of orange lights along the railway arches and the brighter, more obtrusive light of the Strata building, stretching up into the sky. Anything might be moving out there. Anything might be watching.

Something shifted at the upper edge of her vision. Alessa cast her eyes up to the balcony overhanging the patio.

A dark, slender creature stared directly at her, dangling limp from the balcony above. Thin arms hung parallel to the black, upturned disc of its face. There was nothing behind the eyes, no sign of life, but she knew it was watching her. A hot spark of panic erupted in her chest. She realised, as the mouth peeled silently back, revealing that perfect circle of bone-dagger teeth, that it had probably been watching them the whole time.

"Jesus Christ," Tom whispered, and when Alessa turned to face him she knew it was not fear colouring his face a livid pink but awe; he seemed thrilled to finally see one, teeth bared, coiled and writhing in the swell of Alessa's fear. Before she could stop him he was off, through the gaping hole left by the missing window, treading a wide arc around the dangling Shade; his gait, ballerina-delicate, might have been comical if it weren't for those exposed, glimmering teeth.

"What the hell is he...?" Alessa began, but Casey put a firm hand on her shoulder, cutting her protest short.

"Look," she said. "It doesn't even notice him."

She was right. Tom was almost directly below the creature, maintaining a respectful distance the way one might afford space to a venomous reptile. And it seemed utterly unaware of his presence, focused on Casey and Alessa with unnerving intent.

"It's like he's not even there," Alessa said, voice barely a whisper. The creature's undulating, metronomic motion put Alessa in mind of a snake in thrall to a charmer, a slow, deliberate sway.

"He's not scared. It's got nothing to respond to. Shit, I was right, it's the emotional trauma, that's how it senses you." Her breathless excitement was tempered with a stiff-limbed terror, fingers clenched like talons at her sides.. *Are you really as brave as you seem?* Alessa wondered. *Are you just as afraid as I am?*

"Holy shit, Casey, can you see this?" The elation in Tom's voice was unmistakable, the unbridled joy of one who has finally come into possession of his own Holy Grail. Alessa's fear warped inside her, twisting and wrenching in her gut until it formed a tight little knot. *Oh, you idiot*, she thought, staring in disbelief at the way he fumbled with his phone, raising it high as if trying to capture the entire Shade in the frame of his camera. *He has no idea. None whatsoever. He's excited because he's never had to be afraid of them. Doesn't he understand how fundamentally fucked up all of this is?*

His phone flashed, once, twice; a blinding burst of white searing tiny green flecks into Alessa's vision, bright when she blinked.

As if awoken by the light, the shadow-thing - the *Shade* - began to shift. It turned slowly, still dangling from some unseen appendage. Drooping arms drew up, an almost liquid motion. Its face swivelled until it found Tom. Oblivious, Tom held up his phone for a second time.

"Don't..." Casey said, but was cut off by the flash; two bright, consecutive starbursts.

The creature seemed to physically recoil, clearly perturbed by the light.

Tom had just enough time to shout "I got it!" when the Shade wrenched free, slipping off the balcony and down to the patio, rising up before him with impossible speed.

"The bloody *light*," Casey said, reverent.

Its mouth opened, wide and silent; the entire length of its body trembled, long midsection pressed against the ground. It seemed hideously malformed, skull long and narrow and crude in design. The rudimentary stubs of fingers splayed from limbs so askew they seemed dislocated, held at angles that surely could not be natural.

Abject fear twisted Tom's features into something grotesque, and despite the tremble of his limbs – despite the grim, horrified line of his mouth, one hand reached out, slow, as though to touch the Shade.

Alessa's entire body was alive with kinetic energy, muscles screaming at her to *move*, but she couldn't leave Tom here, dumb and mesmerised as the Shade drank in the new, exotic flavour of his fear. He deserved it. For all his excitement, and stupidity, and total lack of understanding, he deserved it, but Alessa's well of righteous anger seemed to have gone spontaneously dry.

"Tom!" Alessa hissed.

Tom yanked his arm sharply back, suddenly aware of himself. "I heard it," he said, voice a low whine. "It was inside my head and I *heard* it, and…please don't leave me here." His eyes never left the creature poised before him. *"Casey! Don't leave me!"*

"Step away slowly, Tom. Backwards. Maintain eye contact. That's it, slowly, come on." Casey sounded impossibly calm. "Easy now. Don't look away."

He followed her instruction, stepping slowly backwards with the jerky gracelessness of a windup toy. Casey was still save for the gentle flutter of her hands, silently directing him step by agonising step. It almost worked. Somewhere out on the main road a police siren whooped into life. Tom turned, peering hopefully over his shoulder.

The Shade lunged, the entirety of its body catapulting forward. And then it was on him; his thrashing arms were caught in the tarry murk of it, pinioned beneath its spidery limbs. Alessa had just enough time to register surprise at how *solid* the creature seemed before Tom's scream tore through her.

"Get it off!" He was caught beneath it, belly-up and writhing as the Shade fought to pull him down, needle teeth grazing the soft, pulsing curve of his throat. Tom's voice was shrill, almost hilariously so. Alessa found herself choking back a peal of hysterical, horrified laughter.

"Fuck's sake, help me!"

Neither Casey nor Alessa moved. They just stood there, dumb and appalled, watching Tom thrash like a drowning man, and there, Alessa thought, was her answer: *are the Shades dangerous?* How stupid were they to think they might have been anything else?

Teeth finally found purchase somewhere low down, spraying a gout of bright blood out onto the concrete. Tom's scream turned to a gurgle. There came the brittle crackle of bone shattering, echoing off the walls of the abandoned flat like a firework. Nausea soured Alessa's stomach. They had to do something. *Anything.*

"Oh god please," Tom sobbed, "*help me...*" His voice was thick and wet, his cheek pressed against the rubble, blood bubbling dark between his lips. His eyes were bright and glassy, hand reaching, fingers splayed. *Move*, she told herself, but she might as well have been paralysed; Tom's dark eyes jerked upwards, seeking the back of his skull. Alessa was not ashamed to admit she was afraid, too bloody afraid to go after him, because she didn't want to end up like that; a red-mouthed puppet tangled up in spindle-limbs and savage teeth.

Occipital, she thought. *Occipital, parietal...parietal...*

The sudden iron stench of raw meat hit the back of Alessa's throat like a fist. For a moment she thought she might throw up; her stomach clenched, gullet contracting, but all that emerged was a loud, undignified bray of laughter. Tears welled in the corner of her eyes. Casey cast a horrified glance in her direction. She wanted to stop but couldn't; the laughter poured from her, drowning out Tom's desperate sobbing.

Parietal...

Alerted, the Shade paused in its exploration of Tom's inner workings. Slowly, it lifted its head, peering up at Alessa with dull curiosity. Its exposed teeth were stained pink, trailing ragged streamers of torn tissue. She felt something *pulling* at the back of her skull, a sharp tug like a hook through meat, and even through her laughter she could taste panic, sharp as copper on her tongue.

"Jesus *shit*," she heard Casey say. Alessa felt the sudden pressure of hands buried in her hair as Casey yanked her backwards; the burn of her scalp pulled her sharply out of her reverie just in time to see the Shade plunge towards her. A firework of pain exploded in the vicinity of her left leg. The Shade's teeth tore through her jeans, scoring deep furrows in the meat of her calf as Casey pulled her away, dragging her into the flat and out of the creature's mouth. It made to follow them but Casey freed one hand from Alessa's hair, fumbled frantically in her pockets. Her lighter was small, the flame inadequate, and for a moment Alessa wondered what the hell Casey was doing. But the Shade drew back, wavering at the sight of the tiny flame. It was enough time for Casey to pull her back out into the corridor. Alessa clamped her teeth down on the inside of her cheek, tasting the sweet-sour tang of her own blood. It didn't help. Her leg was on fire, her head was a swirl of grey water, turning the world liquid.

For a moment, the only coherent thought in her mind was one of dull disappointment: *I only bought these jeans last week and they're already ruined.*

Somewhere on the periphery of Alessa's vision Tom began to crawl across the patio, agonisingly slow, limbs leaden and useless.

The Shade watched them depart, eyes burning bright in the darkness, hazy at the edges as Alessa's vision faded. And they were last thing she saw before she lost consciousness completely; twin beams, like torchlight shining in the depths of a tunnel.

SIX

She woke to the smell of melon shampoo and Golden Virginia tobacco, the comforting pressure of blankets piled atop her. Bright light seeped beneath her eyelids, assailing her nervous system. She squeezed her eyes firmly shut, burying her face into the blankets. Her body felt damp with sweat, which made little sense because she was freezing; her teeth clattered in her skull like a windup toy.

She rolled onto her back, shifting beneath the sheets. There was a transient sense of claustrophobia, one that passed when she slipped her face beneath the blankets and caught the scent of her own sour sweat, her own brand of deodorant. Home. These sheets were hers. She was no longer on the Heygate Estate, no longer lying on damp carpet watching Tom slowly being eviscerated. She wasn't in a tunnel deep underground. She was safe, and they could never find her in here. She decided she was never coming out.

Her heartbeat was loud, the blankets warm and silent as the womb. She felt as though she might be floating, cushioned with amniotic fluid. Lulled by the ragged rhythm of her breathing – *inhale, exhale* - closing her eyes, she allowed herself to sink. It was better in here, away from the light and the noise. She breathed in the scent of home and flexed her stiff fingers, her aching brain desperately trying to recall how she had come to be here.

She remembered Casey's hands anchored in her hair, pulling her from the mouth of the Shade. She remembered the Shade's teeth tearing into her, opening great red rifts in her flesh. Somewhere in among the salt and nicotine and washing powder she smelled the faint suggestion of old blood, inflamed skin.

Her sanctum was suddenly and rudely ruptured by someone peeling back the blankets. A sunburst of light exploded into being; she squirmed, lifting her arms, blocking it all out with her hands but a face appeared, silhouetted. Leaning over her. For a moment, she thought she must be lying in a hospital bed, and this was the doctor come to poke and prod at her. Maybe she'd never left the hospital at all after the bomb. Maybe she'd been here the entire time, festering quietly, dreaming strange and vivid dreams – shadows with eyes and teeth haunting her like ghosts, men with bloody hands begging her to *please, help me*. The idea sent a bubble of laughter up into her throat.

"You're still alive, then."

She lifted her arm tentatively, squinting up. Sharp features came into focus. Damp black hair. Grey eyes, smudged with old mascara.

Alessa sat up sharply and regretted it instantly. The world pitched momentarily like a boat in a storm, turning a full 180 before settling back into something resembling stillness. She gripped the arm of the sofa with both hands, clinging tightly until she was certain she wasn't going to fall. Casey watched her quietly the whole time, poised so as to catch her should her balance fail. She wore a grey t-shirt and a blue bedsheet wrapped around her like a cloak, hair stuck to her neck in wet tendrils. Alessa realised that she was the source of the shampoo-and-tobacco smell. She clutched a half-drained glass of red wine in her hands.

"You used my shampoo," Alessa said. Her voice was thick, her throat raw. It felt as if she'd been gargling with broken glass. She lowered herself gently back down, resting her head on the sweat-damp cushions. "And…you're drinking my wine."

Casey shrugged. "You got blood on all my clothes," she said, plucking absently at the t-shirt. "Puke too, a little bit. It was a total mess, really. I had to borrow your washing machine."

"Oh. Wow."

"Mhm. S'okay. Not like you did it on purpose. I'd consider showering too, if I were you. You smell like a tramp. As for the wine, I have to apologise. I was a bit on edge. Usually I'd go for gin but you take what you can find, right?"

"How did I get here?"

"This is not my beautiful house," Casey intoned. "This is not my beautiful wife." She got up, dragging the blanket with her. Tiny feet poked out from beneath her toga, fragile as porcelain. Her toenails were coated in chipped turquoise paint. "Well, you sort of dipped in and out of consciousness for a bit. I managed to get a taxi on Walworth Road. I

132

explained that we'd been at a hen do and you'd gone a bit overboard on the mojitos. Said you'd been in a scrap. He seemed to buy it. Probably sees it all the time, innit?" She gave a dry little snort of laughter as she searched the cupboards. She pulled out a mug and set it on the sideboard. "He wasn't going to take us initially, not with the state you were in. You were mumbling crazy shit and swaying and I think he thought you were going to puke."

"Didn't I?"

"That was afterwards. When we got out. I convinced him to take us on the grounds that it was a ten minute journey tops, and he agreed on the condition that I keep a plastic bag handy, you know, just in case. I gave him a hefty tip too. I think that swung the deal."

Alessa pulled the blankets up to her chin. "Shit. I'm really sorry."

"Don't be. It's my fault you were there. That's why I'm here now. Wanted to be sure you were okay." Her tone was strangely clipped. She focused entirely on the task of making tea nobody asked for. It was then that Alessa remembered Tom.

She reached beneath the blankets to the place where her wounds ought to be. Her jeans had been replaced with pyjama shorts, leaving her calves bare. The tissue there was gnarled and torn, sticky with clotted blood, but as she pried gently at the ridges with her fingernails she felt no pain. Just a dull, curious numbness, like running her finger over a prosthetic. She lifted her hands back up to her face, examining the powdered crust of blood beneath her fingernails, so dark it looked black.

"We left Tom behind," Alessa said.

Casey said nothing. There was the clink of metal on porcelain as she stirred sugar into the cup. It went on for a long time. Eventually, she brought over the mug and set it on the coffee table. There was a pensiveness in the set of her brow, the hard lines of her face. In the glow of the lamplight it occurred to Alessa that Casey was the kind of ugly that, in the right light, becomes a strange kind of beautiful. Like a piece of modern art, all acute angles and flat planes. An acquired taste, and even with Casey's grey, sleepless pallor Alessa thought she could understand what Tom saw in the spiteful curve of her mouth, the harsh jut of her nose.

Saw. Past tense.

"Are we just not going to talk about what happened?"

"Drink your tea," Casey said, sinking into the armchair. Her tone did not invite argument. Alessa reached out and grabbed the mug from the table. Her arm trembled as she lifted it up. It was disgusting how little strength she had. It reminded her of her father in the weeks before he died, too weak to hold a book, or spoon food into his own mouth. She steeled herself as she brought the drink to her lips, channelled all of her meagre energy into keeping it steady. *It was only a bite*, she told herself, as the muscles in her arm strained under the mug's scant weight. *I'm not that weak. It's not going to kill me.*

How had her dad done this with so much dignity?

The tea was too hot. Her cracked lips stung, her throat contracting painfully as she swallowed. It tasted horribly bitter despite all the sugar, and she must have grimaced because Casey offered her a humourless little smile and held up her glass.

"I crushed a few paracetamol in there," she said, holding the glass to her lips. "It's not exactly a hangover but I have no idea how to treat..." she waved a hand vaguely in Alessa's direction. "Whatever it is that's going on here. I don't think altered consciousness and projectile vomiting are symptoms of shock. My best guess is there's some kind of toxin in the Shade's bite, and you're reacting to it. Are you still running a temperature?"

"I'm freezing."

"You're sweating." Casey shook her head. "You really need go to A&E, but how the hell would we explain it? 'I'm sorry, doctor, I got bitten by a semi-solid creature which doesn't officially exist and now I'm feeling a bit dodgy.' I can't imagine that's going to fly."

"The wound's dry," Alessa said. She pulled up the blanket, revealing her bare calf. Her skin was streaked with dried, crusting rivulets of brownish blood. Her wounds had formed six symmetrical scabs, thick as hide and glossy, as if there were black fluid boiling beneath the surface. There was a clean ring of pale olive skin where the blood had soaked into her sock. Already the angry, swollen flesh abutting the lacerations had begun to subside, faded now to a dark, puffy pink. Despite her fever, she still felt the heat radiating from each individual wound. "How long ago was I bitten?"

"Not long. Maybe two, three hours?"

Alessa blinked. It felt like she'd been sleeping for days; her joints were stiff as old hinges. She glanced at the window and found the curtains drawn, contrary to Casey's earlier advice. Still, the narrow strip of sky peeking through the gap was a dark enough purple to suggest that dawn was not yet approaching.

"They don't hurt." Alessa gently poked at the nearest scab with her forefinger in demonstration. She felt only a faint buzz, like fading pins and needles. She poked again, harder this time; there was sudden shift beneath the skin, the outward ripple of disturbed water from a single, central point. She pulled her hand back sharply. The sensation subsided almost immediately, as if responding to her withdrawal.

"You should probably not do that," Casey said. Her eyes were fixed upon Alessa's leg, wary and more than a little bit alarmed. Her lips were parted just enough so that Alessa could see the yellowish gleam of her teeth. It was obvious that Casey had never before witnessed a Shade attack, let alone the physical fallout. But Alessa thought she could smell the excitement on her, a sour electricity like the air before a thunderstorm. She came here to assuage her own guilt, yes, to make sure Alessa didn't drop spontaneously dead or choke on her own vomit. But she also came here to watch. To observe. To fill the gaps in her own mental notebook.

Alessa's muscles spasmed so suddenly that she almost dropped her mug. She fumbled, slopping hot tea onto the sofa as she searched frantically for an empty surface. Her fingers stung with the heat, but it was a good pain, somehow. A meaningful pain. It brought clarity, certainty. She'd been wrong about Casey, but she understood now. She understood everything.

Casey swept in, grabbed the mug from her, lowering it gently onto the coffee table.

"What's wrong?" she asked, staring up into Alessa's eyes, and the greed of her interest had never been so apparent. Casey was like the medical students who came to observe her dad in his last weeks, drinking in his decline and excreting endless notes, scribbling furiously into their little notebooks; his suffering was an academic exercise, the study of the terminal stages of pancreatic cancer, not the loss of a human being.

"You're enjoying this, aren't you?" A fresh wave of spasms ran through Alessa's arms, up her neck and down her sides, her intercostal muscles pulling taut; her spine arched inwards, a sharp, sudden motion driving the breath from her lungs in one short gasp. She gritted her teeth, forcing the words out between them. "You and him. Were you in this together? Got tired of studying each other so you threw me in too?"

Casey's frown deepened. "Alessa, are you okay?"

"Do I look okay?" She wasn't certain whether it was anger or another spasm which drew her high in her seat, clutching the arm of the sofa, but the way Casey shrank away into the armchair suggested the former. The spasms receded, an outward tide, but a deep ache remained, a slow burn, as though her muscles were full of embers. Her fingers were clenched so tightly she couldn't seem to straighten them.

"You're acting proper weird," Casey said. Not timidly – she could *never* be timid, not with that face, those eyes, but she was alarmed, as if she'd never considered Alessa capable of anger. Her pupils flickered back and forth, assessing, perhaps measuring the likelihood of violence.

Alessa's body slackened. She slumped against the back of the sofa, holding herself up with one trembling arm. Sweat beaded on her forehead, catching in her eyelashes like meltwater. Her hair was stuck to the back of her neck. *I'm disgusting,* she thought, catching the animal scent of her unwashed skin. *Disgusting and pathetic.*

"Put that in your notes. 'Subject was pissed off after being savaged by monster, suggest use of restraints in further experiments?'"

"I'm not making notes, Alessa, Christ almighty. I didn't plan this. I didn't tell Tom to run out there like a fucking lunatic. You think I *wanted* you to get bitten? What kind of mental case do you think I am?"

"The kind who watches her friend being eviscerated and leaves him to die?"

Casey's face darkened. "I didn't see you running in there to help either." She shifted ceaselessly in her seat. "What could I do? Dive in and get myself bitten? Face it, we were helpless. Even at three against one we'd have been slaughtered. That thing was powerful, Alessa, it was..." A gush of wine-dark blood spurted suddenly from Casey's nose, dripping down her chin and onto the collar of her t-shirt, but she just kept talking. "...Maybe he got away. Maybe somebody found him. We don't *know* that he's dead..."

"Casey," Alessa blurted. "Your nose is bleeding."

"Is it?" She raised two fingers to her lips, tentatively exploring. Her ministrations smeared thick, tacky fluid up to the tip of her nose, around the outer edges of her mouth. It was almost too viscous to be blood, too dark, like motor oil. She lifted her fingers away and stared impassively at the mess dripping down her knuckles. And then she was talking again, as if there was nothing wrong, as if there wasn't blood oozing down her face and pooling in the hollow between her collarbones, forming strings between her parted lips. The words emanating from her mouth were English but somehow Alessa couldn't recognise them; they swirled and eddied in her brain, a whirlpool of vowels and consonants and hard glottal stops.

"Casey, stop," she gasped. She felt her lungs dissolving, flaking away like dry leaves.

Casey looked up at her. Her entire chin had turned black now, gleaming like fresh resin. She opened her mouth to speak but her lips were sealed tightly shut. As Alessa watched, breathing fast and shallow, Casey's features seemed to recede, sinking into the pale, hard flesh of her face; her cheekbones protruded, driftwood jutting out from wet sand. Her lips peeled back until there was only the black rim of her gums and tiny icepick teeth, rose-gold in the yellow lamplight.

"It was you." The words emerged in a breathless whisper; she was barely aware she'd spoken at all. "It was always you."

"What do you mean?" the Shade asked. It regarded her indifferently as it reached out a thin hand, ignoring the way Alessa shrank into the sofa, her whispered pleas for it to stop little more than a gasp. Its fingers splayed gracefully across her forehead and she found herself drawn to the delicious chill of its skin, disgusted with herself even as she shuddered in pleasure. "Shit," the Shade said, caressing Alessa's forehead with corpse-cold fingertips. "I think your brain is on fire. Oh shit, shitty fuck, what the bloody hell am I supposed to *do?*"

"Get away," Alessa murmured, but the world was waning, and the Shade was beginning to dissolve. She pressed her forehead into its cool palm. "Don't touch…don't…"

As her eyes rolled back into her skull, she thought she heard Casey calling her name.

SEVEN

She felt the soothing sensation of hands smoothing back her hair. Something cool and damp sat atop her forehead, trailing droplets of water down her face, settling in the creases of her nose. It tickled a little. She raised a hand, feeling along the contours of her face until she found the flannel.

"You leave that right where it is."

She peeled her eyelids apart, searching blearily for the source of the familiar voice. There, perched on the edge of the armchair, was Shannon. Her face was tightly drawn, hands tucked between her knees. She looked pale and exhausted. Behind her, a sliver of silvery, overcast sky was visible between the drawn curtains. Morning had finally come.

"You smell atrocious," Shannon said, without humour.

"Thanks," Alessa croaked. She shifted her limbs. They creaked audibly in complaint. The blankets were gone, she noticed, piled up on the floor beside the coffee table. She was suddenly aware of the presence of an ancient oscillating fan standing at the other end of the sofa. "Where's Casey?"

Shannon's lips pressed together so tightly they blanched white. "If it wasn't for her calling me, you'd probably be in a much worse state right now. Why didn't you tell me you were ill?"

Alessa's mouth tasted like stale vomit, her limbs uncooperative; her bones ached with a sick, throbbing persistence. She couldn't begin to imagine what a 'much worse state' would feel like. Suddenly, she was glad to have been unconscious all this time.

"Is she still here?" A distant memory pricked the back of her mind: Casey, black blood streaming from her nose, coating her face, and those icepick teeth emerging from behind resin-shiny lips. Her eyes collapsing into her skull, irises dissipating into the whites. Hallucinations were not usually a good sign.

"She popped out to the shops about ten minutes ago," Shannon said. "Honestly, I wanted to take you straight to A&E but you fought like a demon. I didn't think you were capable of it in the state you were in but even between me and Casey, it was impossible to get you off the sofa. If your temperature hadn't started to subside, I'd have hogtied you just to get you in the back of an ambulance."

"Was I that bad?"

"I made the grievous error of trying to open a window and you almost flew at me. You were out of it, Ali. Under other circumstances it probably would've been hilarious."

"I don't remember that at all."

"I'm not surprised," Shannon replied. "You were talking total rubbish. Actually, my first thought was that you were high on something. It wasn't until I felt your forehead that I realised there was something really wrong with you."

"I haven't been high on anything since I was nineteen years old, and I'm pretty sure that was dried parsley in a roll-up."

Shannon smiled. "I know, it's stupid. But you've been delicate lately," she said, casting her eyes down into her lap. "I know it's been hard for you, this past six months or so. It's been this sort of…horrible conga line of bad luck. And I just want to cocoon you in bubble-wrap and keep the whole world away from you until you're done healing, but I also know you'd hate me for it if I did. So I've tried to just let you do your thing, and I guess it's been working, hasn't it? You've not thrown yourself off a bridge, or turned to crack cocaine, or run off to Vegas to marry the pizza man."

"I'm glad I've exceeded your expectations," Alessa said dryly.

"You *know* that's not what I'm saying," Shannon said. "I mean, the last time I was here you were basically living in squalor. This flat was filthy. Entire *ecosystems* were springing up in the back of your fridge. And look, you've got washing on the line and I can actually see the floor, and…this is an improvement, Alessa. I don't know if it's the counselling or Casey, or just time healing all wounds like they say it does, but…"

"My ears were burning," Casey announced, entering the room with a plastic shopping bag and a cardboard tray containing two Costa cups. She smiled when she saw Alessa, a smile which reached all the way up into the creases at the corners of her eyes. "Hey, look who's back in the land of the living," she said, lowering the bags and the tray cautiously onto the coffee table. Alessa got a strong whiff of coffee. Shannon rarely touched the stuff, which suggested she hadn't slept since leaving her night shift. Guilt soured her stomach.

"You look a little less on the verge of death," Casey said. "I'm going to take that as a good sign."

"Her fever's down," Shannon said.

"That's good," Casey settled on the edge of the sofa. She was wearing her own clothes again. They must have dried while Alessa slept. "I swear to God, it was like you were fresh out of the oven or something. I could practically see the heat rising off you. I grabbed your phone to see if there was anyone I could contact and you had like nine missed calls from your sister, so I called her back and told her what happened. She came straight over." Casey shot Shannon a grateful smile.

"You told her everything?"

"Well, yeah," Casey shrugged, as if 'everything' were just a normal series of events.

Alessa turned her expectant gaze towards Shannon, who sighed, shifting in her seat. The springs creaked noisily beneath her. Alessa's heart thundered in her chest as Shannon's eyes met her own. *This is it*, she thought. *She'll have to believe me.*

"You met with Casey and someone named Tom at a coffee shop off the Elephant and Castle," Shannon said. She pulled the lid of her coffee, giving it an experimental sniff. "You seemed normal right up until you went outside. Casey says you complained of a headache, but didn't think anything of it. Maybe ten minutes later, after leaving the coffee shop, you passed out on Walworth Road. Casey tried to call an ambulance but you insisted you'd be fine."

Alessa's heart lurched.

"That was around about the time you vomited all over me," Casey added, sipping daintily at her own coffee. "Don't worry about it though. Tom can't hold his drink, so I'm sort of used to it. Getting you in a cab was hell, though. Have you ever tried to flag down a taxi covered in someone else's stomach juice?"

"She brought you back here, and you seemed to be doing okay right up until you had what Casey describes as a seizure - I'm assuming probably a febrile convulsion, considering your temperature was forty degrees when I got here. That's when she called me."

No, Alessa thought, breathless, *you've got it all wrong, Casey has it all wrong, something here is very fucking wrong...*

"You should've seen her, Alessa," Casey said, with a faint grin. "She's got this bag of medical shite with just about everything you can imagine inside – needles, bandages, big plastic bags of water..."

"...saline," Shannon said, by way of explanation. "Which I'm not really supposed to have, by the way, so don't say a word."

"She's probably got a little surgical kit in there too, maybe a foldout travel scalpel and...hey, Alessa, you all right?"

No, she thought. Her eyes flitted between Shannon and Casey, frustratingly earnest in their sudden concern. And there was the panic again, cresting inside of her like a great wave. It was almost a relief to sense it there, familiar as an old friend. "That's not..." she began, but the words were clumsy on her tongue and she had to stop. It hurt to swallow; she felt as if she might choke on the accumulation of mucus and panic in her throat. "What about Tom?" she blurted, and even as the words escaped her mouth she was terrified of the answer. Because either Casey was lying or Alessa had gone insane, and Alessa wasn't sure which scared her more.

Casey and Shannon exchanged glances, mutual alarm evident in the identical trough of their brows. "I don't know," Casey said, a little bemusedly. "I guess he went home? I think he split after you started doing your Linda Blair bit. Alessa, are you okay? You look really bad." She extended a slow hand, palm flat, fingers splayed.

Alessa's heart was a stuttering drum, arrhythmic and far too loud. Her nerves were thunderheads waiting to discharge. She felt very much as if she was about to explode.

Casey's palm was inches from Alessa's forehead when she shot out an arm, catching Casey's thin wrist and wrenching hard. Delicate bird-bones ground in her grip.

Casey let out a yelp, tugging hard, but Alessa was stronger, and panicked adrenaline lent her a power she hadn't thought herself capable of. She didn't want to hurt Casey, but she needed to know what was real, and the smooth, human warmth of the other woman's skin grounded her firmly in the here and now. She was not lying on the carpet in a derelict flat, or stumbling through a tunnel in the dark, or trapped in a tangle of her own blankets while a Shade masquerading as her friend drew ever closer.

"Alessa!" Shannon spilled from the armchair to her feet. "The bloody hell are you doing?"

"I'm sorry," Alessa said. It came out like a sob, and she hated herself for it. "I'm so sorry, but she's lying, and I can't…Casey, I need to know that you know. I need Shannon to believe me. Please tell her the truth. She can help us if she knows."

"Jesus *shit*, Alessa, you're hurting me!"

"Tell her the *truth*."

"What are you talking about?" Casey's teeth clenched in sudden panic, her eyes wide beneath wildly arched brows. She wriggled ineffectively in Alessa's grasp, tugged and writhed like a rabbit in a snare. "What truth? Alessa, let *go*, we can talk properly about this if you just stop…"

"You know what I'm talking about." She could almost smell Casey's fear, bright and sharp like a fresh wound, and part of her *wanted* that. She wanted Casey to know she couldn't mindfuck her like this. "I'm taking about Tom. I'm talking about his guts on the patio. The Shade, Casey, don't tell me you don't remember because you were *right bloody there*."

She heard Shannon approach before she felt her, fingers prying Alessa's firmly away from Casey's wrist. Her thumb twisted painfully. She hissed through her teeth, staring up at Shannon with genuine hurt and surprise. Her sister's expression was as blank as a brick wall, and she might as well have been one, placed between Casey and Alessa, impassable, impenetrable.

"You might be sick, but that doesn't give you free reign to be an arsehole," Shannon said. "Try again, Alessa. Calmer this time."

"Tell her," Alessa implored. Her chest seemed full to the brim with fluid, pressing on her lungs, making it impossible to draw a full breath. "Please."

"I'm sorry, Alessa," Casey said, cradling her injured wrist to her chest. She was visibly shaken but couldn't hide the reproach in her gaze, the anger bubbling beneath the rigid set of her shoulders. *I was only trying to help*, she seemed to be saying. *You didn't have to go all psycho on me.* "I can see how upset you are but I can't just pretend I know what you're on about. Humour me here, yeah?"

Alessa sank back into the sofa. A trickle of sweat slid between her shoulder blades, tracing the downward trajectory of her spine. She looked over at the window, the curtains drawn so as to keep out the light. The perfect dark little sanctum, she thought, as Casey's hallucinatory transformation slipped once again into the forefront of her mind.

"You *do* know," she said, calmer this time. "You said so yourself. Before Shannon came. You said that even if it were three on one, it would've slaughtered us. And then you said we couldn't be certain that Tom's dead. And then..." *and then you turned into a Shade*, she didn't say, and the vividness of that particular memory cast a horrible doubt over all that preceded it. "I think I passed out after that," she finished.

"Why would Tom be dead?" Casey asked, a little too gently. It was the tone of voice people used to talk someone down from a ledge.

"The Shade attacked him! He tried to take a photo, and...don't do this to me, Casey, it isn't fair. Fuck's sake, Casey, if it never happened, how do you explain this?" She kicked off the blankets to reveal her bare legs. She drew her knee up, displaying her torn calf. Shannon scanned Alessa's leg, trying to reconcile her strange injury with Casey's claims. Alessa stared at Casey, searching her face; *how will you deny this? How does this fit into your version of events?*

"Alessa," Shannon said, after a moment. "What am I supposed to be seeing?"

"Look," Alessa snarled, jabbing an angry finger. "Where do you think these came from? You've seen enough bite wounds in your time, Shannon, what do you think these..."

155

She looked down.

The skin of her left calf was smooth. Only a faint bruise remained. Frantically, her fingers scrabbled for the ridge of an old scar, seeking the heat of ruptured skin, but there was nothing except for three days' worth of faint, spiky stubble and beneath that, a purplish splotch which might have been weeks old.

"Alessa…" Casey began.

"My jeans," she demanded. "Show me the jeans I was wearing last night."

"They're right here," Casey said. She pointed to the radiator adjacent to the doorway, upon which a pair of damp, dark blue jeans was slung. The legs were perfectly intact. No rips or tears. Not so much as a speck of blood.

She rose sharply from the chair, startling them both. She swayed a little as she shoved past them both, smelling the sour odour of her own feverish skin as she wrapped her arms around herself. "You need to go," she said, snatching her jeans from the radiator. The waistband was still damp, but she tugged them on over her shorts all the same. "Both of you."

"I can't leave you alone," Shannon said. "Not in this state. You're not well, Alessa..."

"You can do what I bloody well tell you to do." Her voice was shrill as she fumbled with the button fly. Her hands seemed numb, her fingers unwilling to obey her orders. "Just go. Both of you. I can look after myself."

"You..."

"Get *out*." The sheer effort of it made her stumble; the wall caught her weight, and she managed to right herself before Shannon could make a fuss. "If you don't go, then I will. I don't care if I'm sick, I will walk the streets until you're both gone."

Casey's face was pale, expression blank, but her eyes betrayed her heart. She was afraid; whether of Alessa's sudden violence or her fragile condition, or the truth in her crazed ramblings, she was afraid, and Alessa wasn't sure how she felt about this sudden fissure in Casey's armour.

"I'm going to call you." Shannon waved an accusatory finger, eyebrows raised in indignation as though *she'd* been wronged somehow. "On the hour, every hour, and if you don't answer me - even just to tell me to piss off - I'm going to send the police round. Is that clear?" She was still jabbing furiously at the air when Casey finally gathered the wherewithal to shepherd her out into the hall, away from Alessa. When the click of the front door came at last, signalling their exit, she let her limbs go slack, collapsing in a barely-contained heap of limbs and sweaty hair. Nose pressed against the sideboard, inhaling the smell of musty carpet and old paint, she closed her eyes and made the world go away.

*

Time is fluid. Sometimes, she thinks she might be dreaming, and there's a strange freedom in those hazy, liquid moments. The opportunity not to think, or to care, but to observe. To float, untethered, no longer bound to the anchor of her anxiety.

Familiar faces wax and wane, coming in and out of focus. They speak in voices which don't belong to them. Once, wandering dazed past the living room window, she catches sight of her own reflection – distorted, as if seen through moving water – and there beside her, fat and smiling, is her father.

She draws herself up. Her window-self follows suit, moving with the careful slowness of one whose joints are beginning to rust. Her dad says nothing at all. He's wearing the suit they buried him in – grey pinstripe, wide lapels, his Godfather suit, he used to call it. After his death they'd had to alter the suit to fit his diminished frame, but here, in the window, her father is the same abundant, fleshy cask of a man she remembers from before his illness.

He's not really there. Her body realises this before she does; her heartbeat does not quicken, nor does she reach for him. The Shade bite has done something very strange to her brain chemistry, and the boundaries between dream and reality have been smeared like fingerprints on a windowpane. She can't even really be certain that the argument really happened, save for the visceral, physical memory of her hand tight around Casey's wrist. And, strangely, that doesn't scare her. There's a certain liberation in understanding that one's madness has a source, a font from which all her confused hallucinations and feverish imaginings have sprung. The toxicity of the Shade's teeth, running rampant through her bloodstream. Her eyes meet her father's. Whatever strange force is replicating him has neglected to fill in that bright, beautiful spark in his eyes, that vibrancy her father held doggedly onto even as his body slowly destroyed itself. Still, she smiles, pressing two fingers to the space adjacent to her heart, and he smiles back.

"I'm sorry," she tells him. Her throat feels terribly swollen, her voice a watery gurgle. It reminds her of him in his last days, struggling for air even as his lungs filled with fluid. "I've made such a mess of everything."

When the sun peers out from between the clouds, he fades first to a pale chalk outline, and then into nothing. And she folds her aching body onto the sofa, slips her forearm back over her eyes, and lets him go. For good, this time. *Goodbye, dad*, she thinks, the buzz of her mobile on the table rattling deep inside her brain. *I'm sorry I never got to say it to you. I know you understand.*

Sometime later, she wakes curled in the bottom of the bath, the shower head spraying a fine mist of cold water down upon her. Tom is peering over the lip of the bath, blood-smeared and beautiful, fingers curled around the enamel.

"You can't go to the hospital," he says, though his mouth doesn't move, and his voice seems to emanate from deep within the plughole. She scoots sluggishly through the shallow puddle, dragging her heavy skull until her ear is poised over that black hole in the floor of the bath. "What would you tell them?" he asks. "Would you tell them about me?"

She tries to reply, but her voice is lost, swallowed up by the gaping drain. The words splinter, shattering into brittle pieces, and all that's left is an echo, faint and growing fainter as Tom's body shifts, warping like a reflection in turbulent water. And then it's her mother standing there, wearing only a thin, gauzy yellow dress. Her nakedness beneath is startlingly obvious, but she's oblivious, or perhaps she simply doesn't care. Alessa can see everything: the concavity of her abdomen, the vicious protrusion of her hipbones; the space between her legs is as smooth and sexless as a doll's. She's a pale gold spectre standing beside the bath, staring with something akin to pity at her damp, curled-up daughter.

"That girl is dangerous." Her mother's voice emanates from the plughole, and Alessa knows from the disdain in her voice that she's talking about Casey. "She is not your friend. I want you to understand that, Alessa. I'm only looking out for you. You know that, don't you?"

The smell of rain-wet pavement filters in through the open door. *They'll get in*, Alessa thinks, struggling to peel herself from the bottom of the bath, but her mother's firm hands clamp down on her shoulders and she's too weak to fight, sinking down into the water. Her sore, exhausted body relents with grateful ease. *Let them come,* she thinks, turning her face away from the door. Away from her mother. Heavy lids slip down over gritty eyes. She doesn't want to be this tired anymore. She doesn't want to live in fear. If they're coming, let them come.

They don't come.

Alessa woke with a start in the kitchen, holding a half-pint of milk in one hand. The milk tumbled to the floor, spraying out across the lino. Her bare feet left wet track marks; her damp clothes stuck uncomfortably to her skin.

Her head thumped like a bass drum in an empty room.

She rubbed her eyes with the balls of her palms. There was nobody else around, no sign of Casey or Shannon. Nothing to prove they'd even been there except for the complete absence of any stray plates, cups or magazines. Everything was in its place, or at least, the place Shannon had determined it should reside. She had always acted as though she could tidy everything back to normal, induce a state of harmony armed only with a Hoover and a tin of furniture polish.

She got down on her knees and scooped up the plastic milk bottle, laying kitchen towel down on the lino to soak up the milk. It would start to stink if she didn't mop the floor properly, but that was an effort she physically couldn't make just yet. She made to stand, clinging desperately to the worktop with the tips of her fingers as her legs failed spectacularly to propel her upwards. Her brain was an overinflated balloon pulsing in time with her heartbeat. When she finally staggered to her feet she pressed her hot face against the worktop, waiting for the pulsation to subside, or for her head to finally explode.

Distantly, her leg throbbed.

Standing there, spilt sugar grainy between her cheek and the worktop, she searched the dark cavern of her memory for the time she'd lost. There were brief flashes of colour and motion, fragments of sound like an aural jigsaw in which all the pieces were jumbled. She remembered bright sunshine pouring through the window, bathing her supine form in its protective glow. She remembered her father, her mother, Tom's voice emanating from the drain, a sudden burst of fever so intense she had crawled into the bath and lay beneath the trickling showerhead until the wildfire beneath her skin had finally gone out. It was like watching pieces of film spliced together at random, incomplete and nonsensical, and a coherent narrative was nowhere to be found. She had been curled on the hallway floor, and now she was here, and the chasm between those two facts was vast and fragmented and terrifying.

Across the room, her phone vibrated. Slowly, she lifted her head, seeking the source of the sound. It was in the centre of the tiny dining table, hemmed in by clean washing on all sides. She unlocked the phone on the fourth try, swearing under her breath at her own useless hands. Two missed calls from an unknown number. No missed calls from her sister, according to the display. *Shit*, she thought, perching on the edge of the table. She must have answered. Shannon always followed through on her threats, and if Alessa had failed to answer her calls the police would have battered the door down by now. Just what had she said, in her delirious state, to keep her fretful, angry sister at bay?

The time on her phone read eleven twenty-three AM, which startled her – just how much time had she lost? What had she been doing for the last several hours? The gaps in her memory were wide and confusing; she couldn't shut down the panic squeezing her stomach, a too-tight belt fastened taut around her abdomen.

"That girl is dangerous."

Casey. Everything came back to her. She'd thought Casey had the answers. And she did, but Alessa was no longer certain she wanted to hear them. Only a few days ago she wanted to know more, to know *everything*, but now it seemed like enough just to know that the Shades really existed. The rest of it seemed to lead down the rabbit hole, and the more she discovered, the deeper she found herself. Alone and trapped in the dark, with the Shades lurking on all sides, and only Casey for guidance.

Alessa headed into the warm, quiet solitude of her bedroom. The curtains were drawn and pale light filtered through the pink-orange fabric. She stretched out on the bed, easing her tight muscles, the rusted hinges of her joints complaining as her limbs pentacled outwards. She would think about it all later, she told herself, letting her eyelids slip shut. Her eyeballs pulsated in their sockets, dry and hot, and she draped an arm across her forehead, casting a pleasant shadow.

As she let herself drift, she pretended it was summer, and that just outside the window was a glorious turquoise sea rolling gently in to the shore, just like in that poster: the one she'd been staring longingly at a few minutes before the bomb.

*

She felt a little clearer when she woke. Her sheets were soaked through with sweat, but at least she wasn't shivering any more. She wondered if the fever had broken, or if this was merely a lull. The pain in her muscles and steady churn of her stomach suggested the latter.

The display on her phone read 15:41. Maybe she could just go back to sleep, sweat out the sickness. Maybe sweat the madness out too. She could forget the entire thing and pretend everything was normal. Pretend the Shades weren't real. If she worked hard at getting better, would they lose interest in her? She'd have nothing to offer them; they'd have to move on. Find someone new to torment. And yes, perhaps they'd drive that person to the brink of madness too, but at least it wouldn't be *her*.

Alessa dragged herself into the bathroom, holding onto the shower caddy as hot water prickled against her skin. Every part of her seemed to hurt, a dull ache radiating outwards from the smallest of follicles. She'd make another appointment with Moira. Perhaps she'd go back to the trauma group, meet new people. Talk things over. If Shannon had been right about anything, it was that her own stubbornness had put her here. She had to accept the help offered to her.

Her clothes were puddled on the bathroom floor. She scooped them up, intending to dump them in the wash basket. Something fluttered from the pocket of her jeans. A scrap of paper. Frowning, she retrieved it from the floor. It was a folded-up receipt, print faded with age. She stared at it for a long time, hardly daring to breathe, turning it briefly sideways to be sure she knew exactly what she was looking at. It was just a stupid piece of paper, but in that moment it meant everything. It *changed* everything.

The receipt was faded from washing, but she could still see the date: almost a year previous, from the ticket machine at Manchester Piccadilly train station. Which meant the jeans bundled in her arms could not possibly have been the brand new ones she'd worn the night before.

Which meant Casey had deliberately switched her jeans. And *that* meant Casey had something to hide.

Alessa's laughter was utterly silent, vibrating like a marble inside of her skull.

This time, when her mobile rang, she answered.

EIGHT

The sandwich shop was located off Borough High Street, a few minutes' walk from the market, which was almost done packing up for the night. Alessa ordered a hot chocolate, unable to cope with even the thought of solid food, and sat by the entrance. The sun had set, leaving only a bright smear of fuschia on the western horizon. She wondered, with a detached horror, whether her existence really had become nocturnal. Whether she'd be unable to leave the house during daylight hours, if she ever tried. She imagined herself a skittish fox, scuttling through dark streets, shying away from car headlights.

The overwhelming sweetness of the hot chocolate sent a dizzy spiral shooting straight up into her brain. She almost gagged on it, struggling not to spit it back out into the cup. It settled hot and uncomfortable in her empty stomach.

"Oi."

She looked up sharply. There was Casey, standing in the doorway, a huge rucksack strapped to her shoulders. The lighting was harsh on her face, highlighting bruise-dark shadows beneath her eyes. Despite everything she was smiling; there was a brightness in her eyes which suggested it was genuine.

"I know what you did." Alessa said. She wished she had mouthwash, or water, anything to rid her mouth of the cloying, sugary taste. "I found the jeans. The torn ones you tried to get rid of."

"Ah. Yeah. I'm sorry about that." Casey slipped into the seat opposite, dumping her bag on the floor. Close up, she stank of cigarettes and, strangely, of something like rust. "You sort of backed me into a corner there. I didn't want to lie, but..." she shrugged. "Look, we both know your sister would never have believed it. She'd have freaked out, probably. It sounds *mental*, Alessa, that's why you can't just go round telling people about it." She paused for a moment. "Did you really go rooting in the communal bins? I'm not sure if I'm disgusted or impressed."

"You lied to me."

"You didn't leave me a lot of choice."

"I thought I was going insane."

Casey sucked in a breath through her teeth. "I *said* I was sorry," she said, folding her arms sulkily across her chest. "I did it to protect you. To protect us both. Can't you see that? Don't you know what happens when you tell outsiders about this kind of thing? Imagine your sister told you she'd been abducted by aliens, or seen the Loch Ness Monster swimming down the Thames. Would you believe her? No, you'd think she was a fucking fruitcake. What makes this different? And don't say 'because I know what I've seen'."

Frustration welled up inside of her. She pressed her palms against the too-hot mug, savouring the burn. "Even if you backed me up?"

"*Please*, Alessa, she doesn't know me from Adam," Casey snorted. "I could be anyone. You could've paid me to corroborate your story. Christ, I could be the one who put the idea in your head in the first place. I mean, your wounds basically healed overnight, and it's not like we're swimming in proof." She lowered her voice, as if she'd only suddenly become aware of the presence of everyone else in the shop. "It sounds fucking mental,

Alessa, because it *is* fucking mental, and if I hadn't seen the Shades firsthand myself I wouldn't bloody believe you either. I did what I had to do to keep us both safe and I'm not going to apologise for it any more than I already have."

"What about Tom?"

Her eyes darted wildly in her skull like pinballs, gauging the number of people within listening distance. "Not here," she said, which confirmed all of Alessa's worst suspicions. The spilt blood on the concrete, the slick ribbons of tissue spilling from the Shade's wide-open mouth - all of it was real. Nausea rose in her throat and it was all she could do just to shut her eyes and pray that she wouldn't vomit. When she swallowed, she tasted bile laced with sugar.

"I asked to meet you here for a reason," Casey's disembodied voice seemed to be coming from somewhere very far away. If Alessa squeezed her eyes tightly enough, would Casey disappear completely? If she clicked her heels three times would this strange tangle of lies and unbelievable things suddenly make sense? But Casey just kept talking: "I've had a breakthough,

Alessa. I think we really have a chance to end this for good…"

Alessa opened her eyes. "Stop," she said. Casey visibly recoiled at the force of her command, shrinking back like a startled cat. "*Enough*. I'm not playing anymore, Casey. I'm finished with all of it. If you'll excuse me, I need to speak to Shannon. I need to let her know that I'm okay before she calls in the bloody flying squad or something."

"Oh, she knows you're okay," Casey said.

Alessa blinked. "What?"

"I told her you're doing better now." She was utterly nonchalant, almost airy, leaning back in her seat. "I called her a little while after I left. I said you'd agreed to let me come back, and that I'd make sure you were fine. She wanted to talk to you but I told her you wouldn't come to the phone. Don't worry," she added, evidently sensing Alessa's mute anger. "I didn't say you were pissed with her or anything, and I didn't mention anything about…well, you know, this *business*. I just said you weren't feeling up to talking right now, and she said I should get you to call her when you'd had a good rest. I mean, it's only *sort* of a lie. I can see you wouldn't be up to talking to her. You still look like death, if you don't mind me saying so."

"You had no right," Alessa said. It was difficult to speak through clenched teeth, but somehow she managed it. "No right *at all*." Every nerve in her body was alive with rage. How could she ever have invited this person into her life so readily? How could she have fooled herself that Casey was her friend? She wanted to get up and walk out but the sudden rise in blood pressure left her brain numb at the edges; her legs trembled at the mere thought of standing.

"I'm really sorry," Casey said. She sounded solemn, contrite. Alessa knew she felt neither. "But in all honesty, I've probably done you a bit of a favour. You can go back to your sister and make out like it was all the fever talking. Tell her you don't remember saying any of it. She doesn't need to know what really happened. She'd never believe you anyway. People like that can never understand these kinds of things." She smiled encouragingly. Her teeth looked sharp between her thin lips. "Me, though, I mean, I get you. I know where you're coming from. And all I want is to help you. Help us both, I'm not totally unselfish." She gave a small laugh. It sounded nervous to Alessa's ears. She leaned forward, grasping Alessa's sleeve gently with her fingertips. Her eyes gleamed like seaglass in sunlight. "I've found them," she whispered. "I know where they hide. *I found their nest*, Alessa."

It was as if something inside of her had suddenly burst. She felt herself slowly deflating, her spine slackening; she wanted to get up and leave, to lock herself away and pretend Casey never existed but that fierce optimism, that bright spark of energy so similar to the Casey she met just a few days ago had turned her hard-won resolve into powder. Finally, she had the chance to end this. Not just bury her head in the sand and avoid the shadows for the rest of her life, but *end* this.

"We have to stop them then, don't we?" Alessa said. The words were madness, but it was too late to worry about that now. "Because we can't live our lives pretending they're not real. We'll go insane. We have to stop them. We go in with fire. We burn them out." She swallowed hard. She could barely

176

believe what she was suggesting, and yet it made perfect sense. It was the only thing that did. "And then this all ends, doesn't it?"

Casey nodded. "I think so, yeah."

One thing was true: Casey did 'get' her. She'd blown her opportunity to explain everything to Shannon, and that made Casey the only person in the world who understood her. It was an awful, cold realisation, like waking to discover she'd been locked in a dank, empty basement and only Casey held the key.

"All right. Fine." Alessa said. "Where are they?"

"Underground," Casey said.

*

The moon was a faint yellow thumb-smear beneath a blanket of cloud. The shopping centre was shut; wide, unlit corridors stretched out behind long panes of glass, closed shops lining either side, darkened windows like black mouths. It looked as though things were moving in there - amorphous shapes slipping between doorways, curled beneath the benches - and although Alessa told herself it must be cleaners, or stragglers from the top-floor

Bingo hall, she still found herself looking resolutely away, as though to stare too long might make them real. As though eye contact alone might draw them to her.

Casey led her round the back of the centre, where the old railway arches now hosted an unlikely assortment of Latin American food shops and cafes - closed, now, shutters pulled down and secured. A few people lingered, lit cigarettes glowing bright in the dark. To their left was the uplit carcass of the former Heygate development, still beset with workmen getting ready to clock off for the night. Their shouts echoed across the empty, rubble-strewn expanse. It was a strange comfort, knowing they were there. A human presence that wasn't Casey.

The shadow of the railway bridge loomed. Alessa held back; shadows were full of things which could hurt you. Black things with lamprey teeth that hissed and coiled and tore out your entrails with horrific ease. She thought of Tom then, skin smeared with black blood, mouth wide and silent even as they tore him to pieces. She pressed her lips together hard, fighting back the whimper that crept up her throat.

They passed beneath the railway bridge. Alessa felt herself reaching instinctively for Casey and forced herself to stop, shoving both hands deep in the pockets of her parka. Despite the cold a thin sheen of sweat coated the back of her neck, sticking her shirt to her back. Even at this time of the evening the street was relatively busy. Car headlights cut through the night, illuminating worn brickwork. They came to an advertising hoarding, a huge board against the wall of the railway bridge, ancient poster sunbleached and peeling. Below it stood a tall wooden fence, a barrier protecting something unseen. A set of padlocked doors sat in the centre, bordered on either side by a fleur-de-lis of faded blue graffiti.

"We're going in here," Casey said. She placed a hand flat against the fence, affecting such convincing casualness that Alessa almost thought they would stroll through the doors. Until a sudden gap in the traffic when Casey hissed "Over the fence!" voice low and urgent, and Alessa found herself scrambling up, hands and feet scrabbling for purchase. Splinters snagged her jeans as she climbed, sharp against her flesh. She wriggled up and across, pausing briefly atop the fence, breathing hard. When she tried to lower herself down, her hands slipped; she landed in a sprawled heap at the foot of the fence, the accumulated detritus of neglect and rainfall soaking through the seat of her jeans. Casey followed, irritatingly nimble despite the hefty bulk of her backpack, a perfect landing on all fours, cat-graceful.

She pulled herself halfway upright, back resting against the wall. The rusted scaffold anchoring the advertising board to the railway bridge seemed suspended above her, a stark metallic skeleton half-hidden in the shadows.

"See here?" Casey said, straightening up. Set into the moss-slimy wall was a door, somewhat rusted, bearing the legend 'Danger: Do Not Enter.' "They used to hold illegal raves down here, back when raves were a thing. Doubt anyone's been here for a while though. Bad vibes, maybe. Good thing about that is once the ravers moved on, everyone sort of stopped paying attention to this place." Casey placed something solid and heavy in Alessa's palm. "Here," she said, flicking her own torch briefly on and off. The sudden glare burned Casey's illuminated face into Alessa's retinas, green and ghostly. "They don't like light, remember? Apparently these have the power of a million candles or something, so it should hold them off for a little while at least. Enough to buy us time to leg it, if nothing else."

Alessa blinked repeatedly, trying to disperse the eerie afterimage. "What if there are too many of them?"

I'm not afraid anymore, she told herself, though she knew that wasn't entirely true: the fear was hollow, an empty terror she felt inside of her like a gaping hole. And Casey was no longer a comfort. Brave Casey, clever Casey, the woman who never seemed afraid of anything. Who'd left Tom to the mercy of the Shades. Who'd lied to Alessa to keep the secret hers for just a little longer. No, she was still afraid, but it was masked by a bone-weary anger. And that was good. The Shades would not taste anger as easily as they did fear. If she could hold onto that anger, make it her shield...

"I suppose we'll be screwed," Casey replied, shrugging. "It won't come to that, though. I know it's scary, Alessa. You just have to trust me."

"Yeah, well..." glancing over her shoulder, car headlamps casting spotlights against the wall "...you'll have to forgive me if I'm finding it a bit difficult to trust you right now. You've not set much of a precedent."

"I didn't *mean* to lie to you," Casey said. She edged up to the wall, pressing her palm against the rust-streaked door. "It wasn't supposed to happen that way. None of this was. I didn't mean for anyone to get hurt." She turned to Alessa, profile sharp, betraying not a trace of fear. "Least of all you. If you don't believe anything else I say, at least believe that. You matter to me. What we're doing here tonight is to help you heal. Help us both heal. Because we're survivors, right?" She squeezed Alessa's arm with her free hand. "You and me, we'll look back on this someday and piss ourselves laughing at how stupid it all was."

Alessa wasn't sure she'd ever be able to laugh at any of this, not with Tom's desperate begging still so loud inside her head. "Yeah," she said, and the dullness of her tone must have gone unnoticed because Casey nodded towards the door and gestured towards a padlock, severed and discarded in the corner.

"Bolt cutters are amazing things," she said, voice low. "I did that earlier. It's right where I left it. Judging by the all the rust everywhere nobody's been here in a long time. Now, listen, lights on once we're inside. And whatever you do, don't lose this rucksack, because in here..." she patted the canvas. "In here is everything we need to burn the fuckers to cinders. Right? Jesus, I can already smell them."

Her stomach lurched as Casey eased the door slowly open. A high-pitched whine emanated from the ancient hinges, quickly swallowed up by the roar of a souped-up engine out on the main road. Thank god for chavs, Alessa thought. She tried to ignore the ache of her knee joints as she stood.

Casey pulled the door open fully, and Alessa recoiled as the smell of the air inside hit her full in the face; the rich, sweet stink of meat spoiling in a hot room. She fell back on her haunches, turned her face to the side and retched up the meagre contents of her stomach. The hot chocolate tasted every bit as sweet on the way back up.

Casey eyed her with dispassionate interest. "Yeah, I did say you could smell them," she said. "Foul, innit? You can tell when they're around just by the way the air smells. Like binbags left out in the sun."

Alessa said nothing. The acid burned bitter in the back of her throat. She wiped her mouth on her sleeve.

"There's no light at all down here." Casey angled the torch beam inside. Alessa followed its trajectory, keeping her sleeve close to her nose to block out the odour. The walls and floor seemed to disappear entirely a few yards in, quickly turning dark, like the depths of a huge throat. They edged inside, the door swinging shut behind them. "I'm not sure how deep it is. All I know is, this is where they come from. It all radiates from here. The Heygate, the station...I've seen them coming in and out, melting through the door like they're made of nothing. We've got to take a punt on this. Either that, or we spend the best part of forever shitting ourselves at every shadow."

For the first time, she looked thoroughly impatient, and Alessa sensed that there would be no arguing anymore. She'd made up her mind. And somewhere inside of herself, beneath a thick veneer of resentment and apprehension, Alessa knew she was right. Above ground, the Shades were scattered, skittish, and that made them dangerous; down here, in their lightless sanctuary, they might be worse still. But they had to go direct to the source. They had to find the nest and burn it to cinders.

The stairwell smelled of rust. Years of accumulated limescale crusted the brickwork like thick white sores. "Where the hell are we?"

"Back in the 40s, there was all this talk about extending the Bakerloo line out to Camberwell and beyond." Casey's own torch beam joined her own, revealing nondescript brick walls stained pale and mottled; tiny stalactites hung from an arched ceiling, dripping a slow, steady stream of water which seemed to originate from above. Behind them, the door they'd entered through, coated with rust so dark it looked like old blood. Ahead, a set of stairs spiralled down into complete darkness. Alessa swallowed. Her throat felt tight. "They never actually got round to doing it," Casey continued. "It wasn't economical, supposedly. So the project was abandoned. But this..." She spun in a slow circle, arms extended, inviting Alessa to take it all in. "See, they started the actual work on the tunnel pretty early on. Camberwell Station even popped up on tube maps, that's how sure they were that it was gonna happen. They started extending beyond the tunnel at Elephant and Castle. Nobody knows how far they got before the call came to abandon ship. Most people you ask will tell you they never even started. But that's not true. Those stairs you see right over there - this leads down into the tunnels which would have been the Camberwell extension."

"Seriously?"

"No bullshit." She held her free hand up. "Do you have any idea just how many unused tunnels there are on the Tube? I have no idea how far this tunnel even goes. I think it runs under the Heygate and heads towards the Walworth Road. I haven't exactly been wandering around with a GPS stuck to my forehead so I don't have a clue how accurate that is. All I know is, there's a tunnel down here and that's where they've gone to ground."

"Why didn't they just fill the tunnel in? Why's it still here?"

"Insurance policy, probably. It was the 40s. No better air raid shelter than a deep-level tunnel." She placed a sympathetic hand on Alessa's arm. "Christ, I bet you think you're still hallucinating, don't you?" A contrite bow of the head. "I'm sorry. I never wanted to do that to you. To mess with you like that. I really didn't."

"But you did it for both of us," Alessa muttered.

"Exactly," Casey said, a little too brightly. Alessa sensed she had registered the sarcasm and was merely ignoring it. "Come on. It's a long way down."

The thought that Casey had scouted all of this out by herself astounded her. Alessa didn't know exactly where bravery crossed over into insanity, but she was certain Casey had both feet planted either side of the dividing line. She let Casey take point as they approached the staircase. She would not be afraid, she told herself, staring a little helplessly into the darkness, spiralling downwards as if into the gullet of some enormous subterranean creature. She would not be afraid because if they smelled it on her, they would come, and then whatever precarious cover they had would be blown. She would not be afraid because Casey was not afraid, and she might be crazy but she was also in total control. And control was something Alessa desperately wanted for herself.

She had not been able to help the Shades entering her life, but she could make them go away. She attempted to focus her mind on this outcome as they headed downwards, her hand trembling a little as she held onto the banister jutting from the wall.

"Is there another way out? A plan B?" Alessa asked, and even though she spoke quietly she still cringed at the sound, her voice echoing somewhere far below. A shiver ran the length of her, sending her limbs into brief spasm. Might be the fever, she thought, though the air down here was noticeably colder and her damp jeans clung uncomfortably to her thighs.

"The tunnel's blocked off by a brick wall, so you can't access the rest of the Bakerloo line." Casey's voice floated up, almost disembodied as she strode ahead. Walking headlong into darkness as thick and profound as an oceanic abyss without so much as hesitating. She really wasn't afraid, Alessa thought, and in spite of herself she felt a kind of distant awe. "So unless there are other super-secret tunnels down here, that door back there is all we've got."

Alessa stopped walking, pressing her palm to her forehead; a dizzying wave of pressure built up in the space behind her eyes until it felt as if the front of her skull might blow clean open. The constant spiralling of their descent and the stubborn dregs of ill-suppressed fear conspired to turn her brain inside-out. She sat abruptly, one hand wrapped around the railings for balance. Her forehead pressed against her knees. "Jesus, Casey, what are we doing here? They're going to tear us to pieces. They'll trap us both down here and I don't even think I can make it back up these stupid fucking stairs." Her eyes were hot, threatening to spill over. "And you're just...strolling, like we're off to the park and not Christ knows how deep underground in a tunnel *nobody fucking knows about*."

"Hey." The sound of boots on concrete grew louder until she felt a presence beside her, felt a spider-thin arm wind around her back, drawing her upright. She sagged against Casey, resting her aching skull on one bony shoulder. She could quite easily just curl up and sleep, she thought. Down here, where the silence was so heavy it seemed almost physical. She could go to sleep and nobody would find her for decades. Maybe someone might come through that door, many years from now, and find her here – dust-thick bones curled tight, withered skin like old brown paper, an artefact from a past time.

"They're not going to hurt you," Casey whispered. "I will never let them hurt you. But you have to be strong, okay? You can't be afraid. We can do this without them ever knowing we were here, but you can't be afraid. They'll smell us coming if you don't calm down."

Alessa drew a shuddering breath. "That's just a theory."

Casey paused for a long moment, as if thinking something over. Finally, she drew Alessa closer, tugging her slumped body up so that her mouth was level with Alessa's ear. When she spoke, her voice was low and rasping. "Tom wasn't afraid," she whispered. "Don't you remember? He was excited. He wanted to see them up close. And he almost did. I've never seen that before, Alessa, not in all the time I've been watching them. I didn't even think it was possible. The little bastard didn't even notice him until he was almost on it, and even then it was perfectly docile right up until the flash went off. But it didn't attack. Not until he showed fear. Can you tell me honestly that you think it's a coincidence? It was focused on *you*, Alessa. Because you were terrified." She drew away. Her mouth was turned upwards, a faint, elated smile. "Everything that happened confirmed practically every theory I've ever had about them. That they're drawn to fear and trauma. That they're threatened by light. The only thing I didn't predict was what they did to Tom, but shit, how could I have guessed that? They seemed so passive the whole time. And the fire...What happened to Tom was awful, but if he hadn't done what he did I'd never have known about the fire..."

"You're happy," Alessa said flatly. She pulled away from Casey's grip, scrubbing furiously at her eyes with the heel of her palm. "You're actually *pleased* about what happened."

"It's all knowledge, Alessa. You can't win a battle unless you know..."

Alessa got up, limbs puppet-stiff, moving rigid as she sought to put distance between them. Suddenly, the dark was welcome, if only to hide Casey's hurt expression. "Did he know? When you dragged us out there. Did he know what you were using him for?"

"He wanted to see them." She was a silhouette a few steps above, seated and still. "He didn't understand why he'd only seen them once. He came along willingly. I didn't *make* him do anything."

"You used Tom. You used us both, and now he's dead because you just had to indulge your curiosity."

"I didn't know..."

"Aren't you even a little bit sorry?" Alessa took a deep breath. She was shaking uncontrollably now, and a fat bead of sweat traced a path from the nape of her neck. She knelt low, pressing her forehead against the railing; the chill of old metal was pleasant against her hot skin.

She heard Casey get to her feet. "You're angry with me," she said quietly, evenly. "That's good. Anger is better than fear."

"Oh piss off."

"Just listen..."

"I've listened enough."

"Alessa, will you shut *up* for a minute?"

Alessa stopped dead, clutching the railing tight in both hands. Casey's voice seemed to echo all the way down, growing fainter and fainter until it petered out somewhere near the bottom.

"Be angry with me," Casey said. "God knows you have a right to be. I've not been honest with you. But you have to believe me when I tell you I never set out to hurt you or Tom. I just didn't know how to handle it when things went mental. That's all. If you don't believe anything else, believe that, okay?" She inhaled sharply. "Everything I've done, I've done because I'm afraid. They've haunted me for too long. Longer than I know how to deal with. And...I'm just so *tired*, Alessa." She sounded exhausted, then, and utterly lost, small and diminished on the stair; she looked like a frightened child, all fragile bones and paper skull and bird-nest hair. Despite the rage boiling inside of her, Alessa couldn't help but feel a pang of sympathy. "After this is over, you can do what you like. If you never want to speak to me again, I'll understand. But please, let's get this done. Because if I have to spend the rest of my life checking over my shoulder every time I go outside...I think I'd rather throw myself under a train, to tell you the truth."

Alessa wanted to tell her that maybe she should just go do that anyway, but the words wouldn't come. And when Casey walked into the path of her torch she no longer looked like a child; she looked older than she'd ever looked. Old, and tired, and teetering on the very precipice of losing it entirely. The thought of living a life spent in constant fear of something nobody else could even see seemed unbearable, and she knew that she could not keep on doing this any more than Casey could.

"All right," Alessa said finally. She indicated the stairs with her torch, painting a brief figure-of-eight in light on the far wall. "Enough is enough, Casey. Let's get this over with."

NINE

The stairs led out into a cavernous tunnel. The roof and walls were conjoined in one wide, perfect arch, ringed with old iron girders like the ribs of an ancient whale. If there had ever been tracks lain here, they were long gone now; the floor was a flat, narrow expanse of grimy concrete stretching out as far as Alessa's torch beam would allow. It smelled like an old church, of limestone and sour dust and cold air. The sheer sense of space down here was almost overwhelming; the last time she'd stood inside a Tube tunnel, Alessa had been surrounded by other people, by the sounds and motion of them, and the bright glare of train headlights still miraculously functioning. Here, though, there was only her, and Casey, and the quiet scuff of deliberately light footsteps echoing in the blue-tinted dark.

Slowly, they headed into the depths of the tunnel.

Alessa kept her eyes trained on the distance ahead. A maddening paranoia crawled in the space between skin and bone, firing off synapses without provocation. She felt a chill on her neck and told herself it was her imagination. It had to be. There was no breeze stirring down here, not even from the way they'd come. A terrible stillness filled the tunnel, as if it had been suspended in time since the last workers had shut the door behind them. As if something huge and monstrous were holding its breath.

Had this been what *he* had felt, walking alone without so much as a torch to that singular point of light? Had he felt the oppressive weight of an entire city above his head, recycled the same stale air through his lungs? Had he walked into the darkness and known, as sure as Alessa knew now, that something watched him from the darkest corners?

"You're shaking," Casey whispered. Her mouth was grim.

"It's cold." The torch slid in her sweaty hands. *Stop thinking about this*, she told herself, but everything was coming apart now, and when she reached to name the bones nothing would come; she was back in that tunnel, the acrid stench of fried electrics thick in her throat, the obscene sweetness of charred human flesh about her nostrils. Anguished sobs ringing in her skull. She pressed frantic hands to her ears, willing the sound to stop. The torch clattered to the floor, lost in the shadows. She was dimly aware of Casey swinging round to face her, of her mouth moving as if to form words, but there was only that desperate sobbing; she stumbled forward, trying in vain to outrun the sound, to get away from whoever was making it. It seemed to be coming from inside her own head, as though there was someone trapped in there, beating useless fists against the slick arch of her skull. She fell to her knees a few yards away, palms flat on the dusty ground. Somewhere far away, Casey was calling her name.

She looked up.

There, in the distance, was a light; bright and small, a single cat's eye in the dark. And just beyond, barely visible but instantly recognisable: a silhouette, hazy in the headlights of the ruined train. There was no mistaking his purposeful stride, the proud set of his shoulders as he set off in search of rescue. She tried to call out, to warn him, but her throat was closed tight...

"Alessa!"

The sensation of a warm hand on the back of her neck pulled her sharply back into reality. One arm flew up, catching Casey's forearm in a desperate vicegrip.

"Jesus!"

Alessa let go. "Somebody was crying," she said, though as soon as the words emerged she realised how stupid they sounded. There was no bombed-out train, no light save for Casey's torch. The only sound was the rapid, concussive thud of her own heartbeat. None of it had been real. "I'm sorry," she said, tongue thick in her mouth. "I thought I heard..."

"Nothing." Casey's voice was a harsh whisper. "You heard nothing. It was just a flashback. They get inside your head, remember? It's okay. We're okay..." She trailed off, rising slowly to her feet. Her eyes fixed on some indeterminate point in the distance, mouth slowly slackening.

"Casey?"

"There." She raised a trembling hand, pointing at something Alessa could not see. Her torch beam swung up, illuminating something slumped against the tunnel wall.

It looked like a discarded sack, something left down here and forgotten a long time ago. Side by side, uncertain, they approached. She was acutely aware of just how still it was down here, of her own gathering panic, the fear suddenly radiating from Casey like a fever.

Something skittered in the darkness behind them. She marched forward, eyes fixed ahead. *I won't be afraid*, she told herself, though the cold weight in her stomach told her it was too late. When Casey stopped, only inches from the object, hands pressed tight against her mouth Alessa knew she should stop too, but she kept going. Slowly, the bundle came into focus. Grey hoodie. Khaki chinos stained dark with blood. And inside them, inert but somehow breathing, the rise and fall of his chest apparent even in this low light, was Tom.

"Christ," Alessa whispered. "Oh no, no, Tom..." She took a step back, almost stumbling over her own feet. And all around her the air seemed to shift, a ball of pressure welling outwards like a bead of blood; the sensation of a storm gathering just out of sight. She stared down at Tom, unable to speak, and when Casey ran to him she was powerless to tell her to stay back. Casey pulled frantically at Tom's limbs, his face, trying desperately to wake him up. A strange keening noise emanated from her open mouth as her hands found the great glistening cavity at his centre, white bone gleaming in the beam of her torch. *Sternum*, she thought reflexively, staring in mute horror. *Xiphoid process. Ribs.*

That skittering sound again, louder now, closer. Alessa turned, facing the way they'd come. The darkness was a thick clot, a physical entity pulsating to some obscene rhythm. She remembered Waterloo station, the way the tunnel mouth had congealed and warped, Shades spilling out like spiderlings bursting from an egg sac. And she knew, then. They'd smelled her fear and now Casey's terror, hot and rich as blood. Alessa grabbed Casey's shoulder. "They know we're here," she said. Casey's eyes brimmed with tears. Her torch clattered to the ground. Alessa snatched it up, dragging Casey upright with the other hand. "Come on."

"But he..."

Tom's limp-hanging head turned to face them. His eyes were open, staring vacantly up at her, and Alessa knew this was not really Tom but empty flesh. His body seized, arching violently upwards, mouth wide and slack. Her fingers tightened on Casey's sleeve, pulling her away but she stood firm, staring raptly at Tom's boneless, convulsing form. From between his blood-crusted lips oozed a thick black tendril; his throat rippled and bulged, a terrible peristalsis, and he was choking but utterly unaware, gagging reflexively as it squeezed his oesophagus. The thick, wet sound was unbearably loud in the quiet.

"It's a fucking Shade," Casey said, sounding more reverent than horrified. "Christ almighty."

It spilled out onto the dusty stone, liquid at first but quickly attaining form; pale eyes blinked into life. Alessa yanked hard on the straps of Casey's rucksack, but her limbs went suddenly slack; Alessa stumbled back, clutching the bag. She realised then that for all of her sorrow, for all of the tears shed, Casey was enthralled. This was the endgame for her, unintended though it might have been; sacrificing Tom to the Shades in return for knowledge, for intimate insight into the very creatures she had set out to destroy.

Another Shade pushed its way out of Tom's open mouth, wet and glistening as a newborn. How many were in there, greedily feeding off the last dregs of his terror? Still clutching Casey's rucksack, she broke into a run, away from Tom and the darkness swelling behind them, threatening to burst apart, releasing Shades in a great black torrent. She ran without knowing where she was going, or what she'd do once she got there. All that mattered was putting distance between her and them.

She didn't get far.

Up ahead, a light blinked into being. She lurched to a halt, ankle twisting awkwardly beneath her; pain lanced up into her hip and she cried out, a brittle sound echoing off the curve of the ceiling. Bathed in the yellowish glow of this new light, a second body came into view a short distance ahead. It was a sad remnant of a human being, crumpled and empty. The clothes were coated in pale dust, ragged at the edges, but she recognised them as well as she'd recognised Tom's. She'd seen them in her dreams a hundred times, always cast in the headlights of the train as he disappeared alone into the tunnel, deaf to her pleas for him to stop. *So here you are*, she thought dully, staring at the gleam of the cheap watch loose around his desiccated wrist. *All this time, and here you are. What a sad, pointless end.*

There came the hiss of approaching footsteps, strange and shuffling. Alessa turned. Casey walked straight past her, blindly unaware of her presence; she passed by the man's shrivelled body without so much as a glance, head held high. Beyond her, the light had grown stronger. She moved towards it as if drawn, stride unhurried but purposeful.

Alessa's ankle ached miserably as she ran to Casey. "Where are you going?" she asked. Casey's face was pale in the light, lending her a strange, translucent beauty. She did not stop walking even as she spoke.

"It wasn't as if I meant it to happen," she said, voice slow and thoughtful. "That's what you have to understand. But after a while you just...you can't cope any more.

Nobody else sees them but you. You think you're going nuts. And then I found Tom, and you. Especially you. I thought everything would be different. Do you know how it feels, to finally realise that you're not the only one? It's like finding out God is real. It felt like I'd been alone for such a long time, Alessa. That's the only reason I did what I did. It was desperation. I thought I could get rid of them. I didn't mean to hurt anybody, I swear on my mother's grave, nobody was meant to die. I timed it wrong, that's all." A small smile turned her thin mouth upwards. "And it didn't even work, that's the kicker. But it brought us together. I'll always be grateful for that. You saved me, in a way. You made me realise I wasn't insane."

"What did you do? What are you talking about?"

Casey didn't reply. It was as though Alessa wasn't really there, as though none of it really was. She just kept walking, smiling, face upturned to the light. "It's beautiful, isn't it?" she said, a little dreamily. "Like sunshine. Sunshine in a tunnel, how weird is that?"

Alessa looked down at the light. Just a pale yellow glow in the distance, not like sunshine at all. Not like a torch beam, either. There was a certainty in her heart - though she could neither explain nor justify it - that the man who had helped her off the train, who had disappeared into the tunnel and ended up here, somehow, had followed that same light to his death. That, like Casey, he'd seen in that light something that wasn't really there. That *they* had found a way inside his head.

She stopped walking and ducked into a crouch, unzipping Casey's backpack. Inside, a tubular object sat upon a small ocean of glass bottles, duct-taped into a solid, heavy mass. The stink of diesel rose, heavy and obscene. She touched the plastic tube with the tip of her finger. A length of pipe. A length of pipe and a cluster of glass bottles, stinking like a petrol station forecourt. And then she saw the curve of something silver nestled in the front pocket of the bag – a cheap, flip-front mobile phone – and she realised what it was. She'd heard the phrase in news reports, after the neo-Nazi bombings in Brick Lane and Bradford the previous year. But this was the first time she'd ever laid eyes on anything like it.

How the hell would Casey know how to make a pipe bomb?

The slither-shuffle of newly-awoken Shades was louder now, increasing in volume as they shook off their torpor. It would only be a matter of time before they came for her and Casey. She had to act fast. Alessa fished the mobile phone from the bag pocket and slipped it into her own. When she looked up, Casey was a few metres ahead, still moving in that slow, ponderous fashion.

Alessa got up. Every inch of her body ached now, from the deepest layers of bone to the tips of her hair. She desperately wanted to curl up and sleep for a week. Maybe she would, once she was out of here. The stairwell back up to the surface was within sprinting distance. She could still make it down there, if she was fast enough. The pull of self-preservation was a peculiar gravity inside of her, compelling her to run for it, but she couldn't. Not without Casey.

"Casey." One hand grasped the other woman's shoulder. She stopped without resistance, turning wide, glassy eyes up to Alessa. "I found the bomb. I think I have the detonator too. We have to go now."

"It's amazing what you can find on the Internet. I got it wrong before, but I did better this time. The fire will make all the difference." She frowned. "I didn't mean to hurt anybody, it's really important to me that you understand that, Alessa. Do you?"

"I have no idea what you're talking about."

"Five years." She smiled vaguely, but there was a strange sadness about the curve of her mouth, as if remembering something bittersweet. Her shoulder was horribly slack beneath Alessa's grasp. "It took me five years to find someone like you. And look at us now. I didn't mean to use you, but it worked out for the best, didn't it? Draw them to your fear. Get them all in one place. Boom. Gone forever, all of them."

Five years.

It hit her then: the enormity of Casey's confession, like a train hurtling towards her.

I swear on my mother's grave, nobody was meant to die.

Alessa stepped back, reeling. Casey just kept on smiling that wistful smile.

Somehow, that made everything so much worse. Five years. The London Bridge bombings. That was what had driven Casey to desperation. Five years of being stalked ceaselessly by the Shades, believing – as Alessa had – that nobody but her could see them.

"It was you." Alessa's mouth felt numb, her lips struggling to form words. "The bomb. Elephant and Castle. That was you. You set it off. You killed those people." She swallowed. There was a lump in her throat, hard as a stone. "You almost killed me."

"It was a late train," Casey said. She seemed troubled by Alessa's reaction, confused, somehow. "I thought it'd be empty. Everyone was supposed to be off the train, but I timed it all wrong. It was an honest mistake..."

An honest mistake that killed four people and injured dozens more, Alessa thought, but the words wouldn't come. She felt paralysed, just as she had been on that train, with the smell of blood and charred flesh thick in her nostrils. For a long moment she was back there, alone and afraid amidst a sea of churned upholstery and inert bodies, heart beating jackhammer fast. She breathed deep and shut her eyes, and when she opened them again it was not bodies she saw but motion, swift and sudden; a seething mass of Shades forming a thick carpet around their feet. Eyes like pennies, bright and malevolent. They swirled and coalesced, each impossible to differentiate from the other. And ahead of them, pulsating in the dark, a glut of Shades so dense they seemed liquid, a thick and viscous mass of them blocking the tunnel like an embolism.

"This time there'll be fire," Casey murmured.

Alessa stumbled back on clumsy feet, putting a few yards of distance between her and them. She reached a hand out, but whatever Casey thought she could see had her full, rapt attention. The Shades may as well have not been there at all. Casey looked through them, past them, hands outstretched in joyous greeting. In the distance, the glow of their eyes seemed to form a singular point of light, small and bright like the beam of a torch.

Alessa wondered what Casey saw instead.

Casey ambled blindly onwards, unaware or unconcerned. Alessa knew she had only one chance to stop her. She also knew she had very little time in which to set the bomb and get the hell out of here. The Shades were numerous, multiplying before her eyes. They kept their distance for now, but she knew they would tear her apart the way they did Tom, and she would be powerless to stop them. She stood frozen for a second, adrenaline like cold fire in her veins; her legs wanted desperately to move, her muscles taut to snapping, and her mind screamed at her to just fucking *go* but despite everything, despite Casey's confession and the wrongs she'd visited upon her she was still human. Utterly selfish and falling spectacularly apart at the seams, but human all the same.

She checked for the phone. Her heart leapt with relief at the shape of it in the pocket her jeans. She would not look back, she told herself, sighting the lumpen shape of the rucksack a short distance ahead. She would run for the exit, take the stairs a few at a time and, when she was in the open, she would blow this tunnel up and destroy everything. The Shades. The woman who'd invited them into her life in the first damn place. And then, finally, she would be free.

She'd never understood Casey better than in that moment.

Alessa switched on the old phone. The screen flickered into life, displaying an alarm clock symbol in the top corner. A message flashed up on the screen: *Alarm set for 4 minutes*. She realised, with some panic, that she'd activated a countdown. She turned, ready to flee, but a small voice came from behind her.

"Look at us both. You're sick and I'm mad and we're chasing shadows underground. Is this how you thought we'd end up?" Suddenly, Casey sounded mournful, and very young. "Do you think that we'd have been friends, if things had been different? Real friends, I mean?"

Alessa turned. The other woman was a pale ghost, backlit and delicate. The Shades were on her, around her, writhing and coiling around her thin limbs, forming a slack noose around her throat. Tasting her madness, so rich and exquisite they seemed to have forgotten all about Alessa's fear. Casey seemed utterly unaware that anything at all was amiss, that she was clothed in Shades from head to toe. That was the worst thing, Alessa thought, as her throat constricted sharply with sudden, surprising grief, her nose stinging with tears. Even now, Casey still thought it was just the two of them. That they'd be together at the end of it all. And she couldn't hate her, not with her madness on stark display: a ribcage stripped of the flesh and exposed, pulled apart. What stood there was an empty cavity. She wondered, briefly, what Casey had been like before all of this. Whether she had ever been a normal person.

"Maybe," Alessa said. The phone felt hot in her hand, a constant reminder. She had to go now or it would be too late. "Yes. Yes, I think so."

Casey's shoulders slumped with what might have been relief. "That's good," she said. Her voice was barely a whisper. "I'll do better next time. I promise. I'll make up for everything." The Shades rose up behind her then, moving swift and fluid, belying their vast collective bulk, and Alessa ran; feet pounding the concrete, lungs burning, head aching like a festering wound. Her eyes were filmed with tears. She ran hard and fast, focusing on the sound of her shoes slapping against the ground. Beneath it came the sharp, brittle sound of bones shattering and she knew, as sure as she knew that she would not regret triggering that timer, that Casey's struggle would soon be over.

She did not remember clearing the stairs, though as she stood at the top, glancing momentarily down into the silent abyss her calves burned, and her breath came in small, sharp hitches, she knew she would never move that quickly ever again.

Alessa reached both hands to push open the fire door and let loose a cry of frustration as it refused to budge, once, twice, finally giving way on the third shove. Alessa tumbled out into the open, landing heavily against the fence. It shuddered noisily beneath her weight, and she cringed against the wall, holding her breath until she was certain nobody would come looking. The air smelled of petrol fumes and damp brickwork and, faintly, of hot food from the nearby restaurant. For the first time in days her stomach growled at the scent of it, and she was disgusted with herself.

The phone was inexplicably heavy in her pocket, as though it were made of stone. She fished it out, staring at the small silver shape in her palm. The screen was blank. The fire door was ajar, the space inside a featureless sliver of black. She had heard no explosion, felt no vibration as she cleared the stairs. Had it been four minutes? Was there any guarantee it would destroy everything down there? There could be multiple nests, all across the city, hiding in tunnels. All the tunnels nobody knew about, stretching below London like veins deep beneath the skin. The longer she stared at the device in her hand, the more futile everything seemed. Casey's plan was short sighted, borne of fear and based on so many assumptions that there were a hundred ways it could fail.

But she had to believe. Because it was all she had left, and because a paper-thin plan was better than no plan at all. Because the very possibility of any kind of closure at all revolved around Casey's stupid fucking bomb.

Slowly, she got to her feet. Her legs wobbled beneath her but somehow she managed. The street beyond the hoarding was dark and quiet. Somehow, she found the energy to push the fire door shut and scramble clumsily back over the fence, hauling herself up with weak, aching arms. Her feet scrabbled helplessly at the wet wood. She landed heavily on the other side, sprawled on hands and feet. Passing cars drove on in blissful ignorance. A small cluster of people walked by on the opposite side of the road, talking in loud voices and gesturing at something Alessa couldn't make out. If they'd noticed her, they hadn't batted an eyelid. It was late. She was probably drunk.

She stood there for a moment, breathing hard, willing herself to stay upright for just a little bit longer. When she finally found the courage to look back – sending out a whispered little prayer, trite and useless: *I wish things had been different too* – she thought she could feel the ground beneath her tremble, just a little bit.

The world carried on, oblivious.

Alessa closed her fingers around the phone and set out in the direction of home. When she passed the hoarding - head down, breathing white in the evening chill – she did not look up at the door. Hot tears streamed freely down her cheeks, dripping salt into her open mouth. She walked on, beneath the railway bridge, out into the shadow of the Heygate building site, and for the first time in what felt like forever, she was not afraid of the dark.

Acknowledgements

I could probably fill up another novella's worth of pages with all the people I want to thank, but at the risk of prattling on (and possibly forgetting someone important) I'll try to keep it short & sweet.

First and foremost, a big thank you to Johnny Mains, without whom this novella would not exist at all.

To Rosanne Rabinowitz, Joanna Horrocks, Gary Couzens (my constant First Reader) and Ray Cluley, for reading this in its various iterations and making it a better story. (Thanks also to Ray for the wonderful cover quote, for which I am humbly grateful). And thank you to Jim McLeod for supporting this book over on Ginger Nuts of Horror.

Thanks always to my lovely, supportive husband Rob, who never complains when I disappear off into the Black Hole of Authordom (and to the makers of Overwatch, for ensuring his continued entertainment). And to my large, chaotic and lovely family, who have always encouraged my writing - from those very first poems right up until today - and who would probably have had every right to tell me to go play with Barbies instead like a normal kid.

To Heidi Squire and Elizabeth James, my English teachers at Bacon's College, who seemed to think I had it in me, and won't be in the least bit surprised to learn that Laura Mould grew up to write horror stories.

And thanks to my friends inside & outside of the writing world, including (but not limited to) Sarah Patten, Violet & Rosie Casselden, the Funcon crew (who send me beautiful postcards & put up admirably with my ability to speak at length about total rubbish), those I've had the privilege of meeting & chatting with at Fantasycon and those I hope to meet at future events – I'll be here all day if I name you all individually! You all know who you are, and you're all brilliant. Thanks as well to my Twitter friends for all the conversation and support, even when I'm being insufferable. Writing is a lonely business and it's infinitely improved by cultivating friendships with those who understand what it's like to spend most of your time conversing with the fictional people inside your head.

And last but definitely not least, thanks to Ross Warren and Anthony Watson for taking a chance on this novella, and to Peter Frain for the brilliant cover art.

SLAUGHTER BEACH

BENEDICT J JONES

When glamour photographer William Marshall charters Dan Curtis' boat *The Ariadne* for a photo-shoot on a remote tropical island it's an offer too good to turn down. Beautiful scenery, beautiful girls… what could possibly go wrong?

The island hides a deadly secret though and soon Don, the photographers and models find themselves in a terrifying game of cat and mouse with a deadly adversary where death lies in wait behind every tree and boulder.

Slaughter Beach – where paradise becomes a blood-drenched hell.

DARK MINDS NOVELLA 1

WHAT THEY FIND IN
THE WOODS

GARY FRY

When Dr Matthew Cole supervises Chloe Linton's university research on a 16th Century warlock named Donald Deere, he is sceptical. Surely it's just a local legend intended to scare people. But as Chloe develops her research, Matthew becomes embroiled in sinister events. They are both drawn into the woodland where Donald Deere was supposed to reside. And what they find might tear apart their minds.

DARK MINDS NOVELLA 2

KIDS

PAUL M FEENEY

Matt and Julie head to her parents' big, remote house in the country, with their children Kayleigh, Carol and Robert, for a day out with friends and family. They intend spending the warm, summer's day doing nothing more strenuous than engaging in light, casual conversation, eating lunch and drinking tea, while the kids play in the background.

At least, that's the plan…

The kids disappear, only to return utterly, fundamentally changed. Something bad has happened to them, something *very* bad.

The day becomes a pitched battle between the adults and the violent psychopaths their children have become. How can the adults survive against such an enemy, how can they even fight back, when the very thing they have to fight against is their own flesh and blood?

DARK MINDS NOVELLA 3

RUIN

RICH HAWKINS

These are the dark days, a time of ruin.

It began when the black rocks fell to earth, bringing with them a contagion which affected man and beast alike, spreading death and destruction across the land.

These are the days of the blight.

The south of England has become a quarantine zone, separated from the rest of the country by a huge wall, a wall Gus Abernethy must cross to find his son Tom, taken from him at the outbreak of the Blight. Amid the decaying remnants of civilisation, Gus discovers he is not the only one searching for Tom, so too are the Nephilim, once human but now changed by the Blight into something monstrous who want the boy for their own deadly reasons.

So begins one man's quest, a nightmare journey in which finding his son really could be the most important thing in the world...

DARK MINDS NOVELLA 4

Printed in Great Britain
by Amazon